"You'd think that after all this time we'd be able to talk about this and get somewhere without trying to throw blame around."

Lawrencia shrugged her slender shoulders at her husband. "Well, maybe that's why we're having trouble."

"I don't get it," Ivan admitted with a slight shake of his head.

Rencia smoothed her hands over her bare arms and shrugged again. "I guess it's gonna take us a while to get to know each other again. You know? Maybe *then* we can talk."

Ivan pushed one hand into his pocket and sighed. "You got any suggestions on how we should get to know each other?" he asked.

"A few. We can discuss them, if you're up to staying another night?" she asked, her eyes narrowing in a look that combined innocence and seduction.

"That sounds good," Ivan began slowly, "but I don't think I can stand another night of sleeping under the same roof with you in a different room," he confided, favoring her with his dimpled smile.

Rencia smiled as well before she turned and headed up the stairs. "Who said anything about different rooms?" she asked, just as she walked past him.

Midway up the curving stairway, she turned to see if he had decided to follow her. He had.

BOOK YOUR PLACE ON OUR WEBSITE AND MAKE THE ARABESQUE ROMANCE CONNECTION!

We've created a customized website just for our very special Arabesque readers, where you can get the inside scoop on everything that's going on with Arabesque romance novels.

When you come online, you'll have the exciting opportunity to:

- View covers of upcoming books

- Learn about our future publishing schedule (listed by publication month and author)

- Find out when your favorite authors will be visiting a city near you

- Search for and order backlist books

- Check out author bios and background information

- Send e-mail to your favorite authors

- Join us in weekly chats with authors, readers and other guests

- Get writing guidelines

- AND MUCH MORE!

Visit our website at
http://www.arabesquebooks.com

Finding *Love* Again

To Yasmin,

AlTonya Washington

Enjoy the romance!

AlTonya Washington

ARABESQUE
★BET BOOKS™

BET Publications, LLC
http://www.bet.com
http://www.arabesquebooks.com

ARABESQUE BOOKS are published by

BET Publications, LLC
c/o BET BOOKS
One BET Plaza
1900 W Place NE
Washington, D.C. 20018-1211

All Kensington Titles, Imprints, and Distributed Lines are available at special quantity discounts for bulk purchases for sales promotion, premiums, fund-raising, and educational or institutional use. Special book excerpts or customized printings can also be created to fit specific needs. For details, write or phone the office of the Kensington special sales manager: Kensington Publishing Corp., 850 Third Avenue, New York, NY 10022, attn: Special Sales Department, Phone: 1-800-221-2647.

First Printing: October 2004
10 9 8 7 6 5 4 3 2 1

Printed in the United States of America

ACKNOWLEDGMENTS

To LaWanda Washington, the author of "Love Changes." Thank you for creating this poem especially for my book.

To the book clubs and readers who have shared your thoughts and invited me into your meetings. Special thanks to Prominent Women of Color Book Club in Jacksonville, Florida, the Camden County Page Turners in Saint Mary's, Georgia, and SistaGirl Book Club in Virginia Beach, Virginia. You're all wonderful ladies!

To the people of Florence, South Carolina: your support has been phenomenal. Thanks!

Prologue

Soft conversation mingled with the cool, jazzy rhythms flowing throughout the spacious lower level of Ivan and Lawrencia DeZhabi's Brooklyn home. The cozy, elegantly furnished brownstone had been the site of many gatherings, and the one that evening promised to be another success.

The DeZhabis' annual Triple Days Mingle was in high gear. The event was always held two weeks before Halloween and was a preview of the festive season around the corner. Although the event occurred well before Thanksgiving and Christmas, it never failed in its promise to fill its guests with joyful anticipation for the holiday season. Of course, there was always just enough business mixed into the festivities.

"Is everyone okay over here?" Lawrencia asked, her green eyes sparkling with the sweetness she always exuded.

Maurice Stiles patted Rencia's hand and favored her with his even-dentured grin. "My love, you are by far the most perfect hostess I have ever seen. And I say that because I'm never satisfied. Tonight, however, I find that I have nothing to complain about."

The group surrounding Maurice joined him in laughter. "Uh-oh, Rencia, believe me, by tomorrow morning he'll even be complaining about that!"

Rencia waved her hand toward Maurice's assistant, Wynette Groves. "Wynette," she playfully called in a hushed tone. "Maurice, thank you very much for the compliment. That coming from a renowned professional such as yourself, I feel even more proud of my little party."

"I always tell the truth, my dear," Maurice proclaimed, tossing back a bit more of his vodka and water.

"Well, you all just yell if you need anything," Rencia called, already spotting more guests who required her attention.

From across the room, Ivan DeZhabi's ebony stare followed his wife as she reveled in her role as hostess. Rencia had decided to handle the party herself instead of letting her husband hire outside help. Ivan was thinking of a way to thank her for including his clients and colleagues in the preholiday celebration.

"I would not be telling you this if I didn't think you could excel at it. You should take this opportunity very seriously."

Rencia's long lashes fluttered as she shook her head. "I appreciate your confidence in me, Maurice, but don't you think you're making a bit too much out of a moderately successful party?"

"Moderately successful, bah!" Maurice scoffed with a wave of his hand. "I have been in this business long enough to know that you have what it takes."

"Has what it takes for what?" Ivan inquired when he approached the cozy duo.

Rencia looked over her shoulder and smiled up at her husband. "Maurice is trying to convince me to come on board as his newest protégé," she explained, snuggling back against Ivan's tall, solid frame.

"Protege?" he queried, eyeing the older man with heightened interest.

Maurice laughed. "Your wife is far too modest, Ivan. She could come on board as a full associate, planning and overseeing her own parties."

Ivan smoothed his big hands across Rencia's arms, left bare by the silver-gray spaghetti-strapped gown. "Sounds like you have a fan, Larry."

"And I appreciate your confidence in me, Maurice."

Maurice poised his glass in the air. "Then, you'll consider it?"

"Maurice—"

"Listen to me, lovely," Maurice soothed, patting her cheek, "I know that you didn't expect to receive a job offer tonight, so take some time to think it over. This big guy behind you has my number. Contact me once you've reached a decision."

Rencia let her eyes close briefly. "Thank you," she whispered.

Maurice smiled. "Ivan," he said with a nod, before walking away.

Ivan's pensive stare followed his client's departure. "Why didn't you just go on and put the old man out of his misery?" he asked, squeezing his wife close.

Rencia shrugged, her green stare following the trail of her fingers across the back of Ivan's hand. "I don't know. I mean, I did say I'd think about it, so . . ."

"Larry, are you taking Maurice seriously?"

"Well, he is a very respected man in his field," Rencia argued, her soft voice taking on a vaguely defensive tone. "Who knows? I mean, perhaps I could be successful at—"

"Larry? Baby, please don't let Maurice fill your head

with a bunch of fantasies. He talks a very good game, you know?"

"Oh, Zhabi." Rencia sighed, tilting her head back and up in order to plant a kiss on his square jaw. "Why are you getting so riled up over this?"

"I'm not getting riled up," he lied, "but to let Maurice Stiles get *you* riled up about a job offer made because he's enjoying your party is crazy."

Rencia rolled her eyes as she turned to face her husband. She let her fingers toy in his gorgeous mane of silky jet-black twists. "Zhabi, for your information, I'm not interested in Maurice's offer, but I didn't want to have to disappoint him tonight. Not when he's having so much fun."

"Thank God," Ivan breathed, his head bowing slightly. He gathered her closer and buried his handsome face in her curly, waist-length brown tresses.

"No, I don't think arranging parties is for me. I'd like to try finding something a bit more challenging," she said, winding her arms about her husband's neck. "Can you think of something more challenging for me to do?" she whispered, her sparkling gaze adding to the suggestive tone of the question.

Ivan mirrored his wife's seductive stare with one of his own. "Oh, I think I can come up with a few things," he promised, joining in when he heard her laugh.

Chapter One

Dozens of male heads turned toward the front of the dining room when the two young women stepped into the Shellfish Restaurant. Casey Franklin and Lawrencia DeZhabi caught and held the attention of practically every man there.

"Mitchell, do you have a table for us?" Casey asked, over the volume of various conversations filling the dining room.

Mitchell Sykes pretended to be aggravated by the tall, dark-complexioned beauty. "Did you make a reservation?" he asked.

Casey ran one hand across her short, neat Afro. "Reservations? For a seafood bar? Please!"

Mitchell took Casey's arm in a firm yet playful hold and pointed his index finger a few inches from her small nose. "Keep comin' in here insulting my establishment and I'll kick you right out," he threatened.

"Oh . . . well, that's fine," Casey challenged nonchalantly. "But let Rencia stay, she really has a craving for shrimp."

The threesome finally broke into laughter. Mitchell and Casey always teased each other mercilessly whenever they saw one another.

Rencia leaned close to Mitchell and patted his arm.

"Forget her, Mitch. She's been running around all day trying to get a jump on her Christmas shopping. Besides, she's about ready for another birthday so you know how she can get," she excused her friend, mischief making her eyes twinkle.

Mitchell closed his eyes and nodded. "Oh, now I understand. Mmm-hmm, judging from the looks of her, I figured it was about time for another birthday."

Casey fixed both her friends with aggravated looks. "Will you just shut up and give us a table?" she ordered Mitchell.

"Damn, Case, gettin' kind of testy in your old age?" he asked, ducking when she swatted at his head.

The three old friends were a hilarious sight to behold as they rolled with laughter. Mitchell had to grab a napkin from behind the host's stand and wipe his eyes.

"Come on," he said, stepping between the two leggy beauties. "I figured Casey would pull something like this, so I kept a table free," he said, escorting them through the restaurant.

Casey's eyes narrowed. "Still joking, I see. Lemme find a knife."

Interested glances were constantly thrown toward the two striking women as they laughed with the proprietor. Rencia and Casey always caused a stir wherever they went. Aside from complementing each other's personalities perfectly, their eye-catching features were a tribute to the breathtaking diversities of black women.

Rencia was tall, like her friend, but with a bouncy mane of curly light brown hair that almost reached the small of her back. Her flawless honey complexion, green eyes, and full, pouty mouth were features that left many speechless.

Of course, Casey was no less striking. Long ago, she'd

cut her lengthy tresses into a short Afro. The style had always brought her several compliments and emphasized her naturally seductive looks. In contrast to her friend, she possessed a flawless mocha complexion and hazel eyes that could be warm one minute and snapping the next. Needless to say, both women carried a confidence impossible to miss, yet their open personalities spoke volumes. Neither took herself too seriously.

"Is this the best you could do?" Casey berated Mitchell as she eyed the table with pretend disgust.

Mitchell sighed and turned to Rencia. "I'm sorry, Ren, but I have other customers to think about and if I sit y'all in the middle of the place, Casey's likely to drive everybody out," he explained with a straight face.

Rencia laughed, watching Casey smack Mitchell on the back of his neck. He walked away, grumbling below his breath.

"You and Mitchell are too much." Rencia chuckled as she sat down and selected a menu from the brass holder in the center of the table.

Casey waved her hand. "Hell, he's got to learn he can't step into the ring with me!" she bellowed.

Rencia lowered her eyes. "I don't know, you two seem pretty comfortable being in the ring together.

Casey's eyes widened to the size of small moons. "Mitchell? Mitchell Sykes? Please!"

"Oh, what? He's gorgeous!" Rencia argued. "And he's gonna own this place one day." She leaned forward and pinned Casey with a serious stare.

Casey frowned. "So what?"

Rencia pretended to be in shock. "Girl! You'll never want for shrimp another day in your life," she whispered.

Casey burst into laughter. "You are seriously disturbed, Rencia. Seriously."

Rencia wiped the tears of laughter away from her eyes. A solemn expression clouded her beautiful face. "Disturbed, huh? Yeah, lately I've been thinking the same thing." She sighed, placing a few gaily colored shopping bags on the empty chair to her right.

Casey caught the strange tone in her friend's voice and looked up. "What's that supposed to mean?"

Rencia sucked her teeth out of habit and grimaced. "Nothing. Just forget I said that."

"The hell I will. What's going on with you?" Casey insisted.

Rencia toyed with a curl that had been dangling across her eyes. "I'm just tired of this, that's all."

Casey leaned back in her chair. "Well, if you didn't want to have lunch you could've said something."

Rencia shook her head. "I don't mean that," she clarified with a wave of her hand. "I'm just sick of not having a career of my own. Something to do with my day, you know?"

Casey smiled and patted Rencia's hand. "Sweetie, is that all? Shoot, having a career is not impossible," she assured her friend.

Rencia gave her a sour look. "Oh, I know that," she replied, thinking of the catering associate's position she'd passed on.

Casey had struggled her way through grad school while working. She was now a highly paid financial adviser in New York and wasn't put off a bit by Rencia's pessimistic outlook. "Honey, you can do anything! The sky's the limit," she declared.

"You're right about that. I *could* be doing anything. Would you believe I just turned down an offer?"

Casey was intrigued. "An offer? To do what?"

Rencia smiled as an image of Maurice Stiles filled her

mind. "One of Ivan's clients runs a catering, party-planning business. Anyway, he attended the Triple Days Mingle and offered me a position as one of his associates."

"Well, girl, that's wonderful!" Casey raved, clapping her hands.

Rencia smirked. "Yes, I'm sure it would have been."

"They why'd you turn it down?"

"I told Ivan I wasn't interested in it. That I wanted something more challenging."

Casey smoothed her hands across the tailored olive suit coat and fixed Rencia with a probing look. "Now, why do I get the feeling that you weren't being completely honest with your husband then?"

"Because I wasn't," Rencia replied without hesitation. "The evening was just so perfect and I didn't want anything to spoil it. Besides, me working for one of Ivan's clients? I think I'd be borrowing more trouble than the job is worth."

"Mmm," Casey grunted as she considered the speculation. "You may have a valid point there."

"Which only leaves me in my same tight spot." Rencia sighed, fiddling with a springy coil of her light brown hair.

Casey smacked her palm against the table. "Damn it, girl, why should it?"

Rencia smiled at Casey, grateful for her confidence. "Thank you, hon. It's good to know you're on my side."

Casey shrugged. "Always. But why do I get the feeling that I'm the only one on your side?" she asked, watching Rencia look away in unease. When she shook her head and said nothing, Casey frowned. "Have you even really talked to Ivan about this?"

The mention of her husband in relation to her working made Rencia shake her head again.

"Why not?"

She sat back in her chair and regarded Casey with surprise. "Why in the hell are you asking me that when you know the answer?"

"Girl, besides the night of your party, have you even brought it up? Even vaguely?"

"Casey, you know how Ivan can be. Whenever I ask for his input, he refuses to talk about it. It's obvious that he has a real problem with my wanting to work."

Casey slammed her fist on the table. "This is about what you want," she said, growing furious.

Rencia couldn't deny Casey's observations. Still, it didn't negate the fact that she had a double whammy against her: no job prospects and no support from her husband.

For a moment, she pondered her predicament. In all fairness, she had to admit that her life was near perfect. She had a gorgeous, sexy giant for a husband and he treated her like a queen. True, he had issues about her joining the workforce, but she could never doubt his love for her.

Until recently, she never really even thought about having a career. Ivan was on the road to success with his chosen occupation and could possibly start his own company soon. Rencia found that she craved the same type of success he'd garnered. Being her own person was a thing she was beginning to want more and more.

"Rencia? Rencia, girl, snap out of it," Casey was calling to her a few moments later. "Did you hear what I said?"

Rencia scratched at her eyebrow and frowned her response to Casey across the table.

"Have you ever thought about working for Ivan?" she

repeated, receiving long loud laughter from Rencia. Casey propped her chin in her palm and waited for her to finish.

"Casey, I appreciate all these suggestions, but don't you think that's taking it a bit too far?"

Casey rolled her eyes. "Look, it's better than nothing and you'd be getting experience. Plus, I'll bet he'd give you a glowing reference," she teased.

"Sorry, Case, but asking *your* cousin to be his secretary over a candlelight dinner doesn't seem like a good idea," Rencia retorted sarcastically.

Casey's brows rose impressively as she rolled her eyes away from Rencia. "Damn, forget about candlelight and ask him now."

Rencia followed Casey's gaze and spotted the tall, strikingly handsome man walking into the dining room. Ivan DeZhabi always drew attention to himself. His easy unhurried stride said more about him than any words ever could. It was slow, yet purposeful, almost stalking.

A young man well on his way to becoming a major force in the competitive world of advertising and public relations, Ivan was used to control in both his professional and personal life. His soft, deep voice could send chills down a person's spine as easily as it could warm a heart.

Rencia could feel her own heart race as it always did when she looked at Ivan. His fiercely gorgeous looks captivated her as they did every other woman in the room. A mixed heritage from his Nigerian father and Egyptian mother created his magnificent features. Ivan had the same flawless honey-toned complexion as his wife, but his coloring was much darker. Thick, jet-black hair almost reached his shoulders in a mass of silky twisted locks. The beautiful coal-black eyes deep-set beneath sleek dark brows were unforgettable.

Rencia closed her eyes and bowed her head. "I can't," she whispered.

Casey frowned and stabbed the table with her fork. "Girl, when are you gonna stop lettin' Ivy bully you?"

"He doesn't . . . bully me," Rencia argued weakly.

"Hmph," Casey grunted. "It's more than obvious that you're afraid to stand up to your own husband."

In response, Rencia raised her hand, signaling Casey to stop.

Of course, Casey had more to say. "Honey, I think it's admirable the way Ivan wants to take care of you. There are plenty of black men out there like him, but they're hard to find. Believe me, I know. Still, it's pretty clear you're not happy and that's not fair."

Rencia shrugged. "I'm ready to go," she decided, standing from the table.

"Coward," Casey mumbled, watching her friend don a tanned leather jacket.

Rencia raised her eyebrows and pulled her thick hair out of the jacket's collar. Suddenly she felt a hand on her upper arm and she was turned around. Ivan pulled her into his arms and delighted her with a thorough kiss. Rencia moaned instantly, her fingers curving around the lapels of his salt-and-pepper suit coat. The fact that the restaurant was crowded mattered little to Ivan as he lavished his wife with a slow, deep kiss.

Ivan finally released Rencia, a devious smirk crossing his mouth when he glanced past her. "What's up, Case?" he greeted, his dark eyes twinkling with mischief.

Casey shook her head as she grinned at her first cousin. Though she wanted to kick him most of the time for being such an arrogant know-it-all, she loved him a lot. Of course, the feeling was mutual.

"What's with the serious faces?" he questioned his wife and cousin, watching them closely.

"Well—" Casey started.

"We were just discussing one of our friends. She's, um, going through some pretty serious stuff. You know, with the holidays and all," Rencia quickly explained.

Ivan studied his wife for a moment longer, before deciding to let it go. Instead, he kissed her again and stepped back.

"So, um, what are you doing here?" Rencia teased, knowing it was often impossible to drag him from his office during the day.

Ivan massaged his jaw while tilting his head forward. "Meeting with Jeff," he said, referring to one of his coworkers.

"So, I'll see you at home," he added, brushing his thumb across the small smudge of lipstick at the corner of Rencia's mouth.

Rencia smiled and watched him walk away, before turning back to Casey. "Don't," she warned, her green gaze brooking no argument.

"I don't want to hear it! I mean that, Silas! You find my girl and you find her now!"

Silas Timmons shook his head as he held the door open for the petite, dark-complexioned woman who rushed inside the Shellfish.

An air of royalty surrounded Geneva Arnold, CEO of GeFran Cosmetics. Geneva and her husband, chairman of the board Franklin Arnold, founded the company before they were married. Now the corporation, which specialized in skin-care products and cosmetics with the African-American market in mind, was one of the largest companies in the industry.

"Kent, don't you have any new faces?" Frank Arnold was asking their head photographer.

Kent Daniels looked completely bewildered. "Mr. Arnold, you've seen every one of the latest shots. They're all new faces."

"Well, they don't look new," Geneva chimed in. "To promote this fragrance, we need someone fresh and captivating."

"In other words, wide-eyed and innocent?" Kent asked, his tone vaguely sarcastic.

Geneva shook her head. "Not wide-eyed, seductive," she clarified. "A woman who is unconsciously seductive. Someone who wears breathtaking beauty with a confidence that says she knows she'd be just as beautiful without it."

Kent cleared his throat. "Well, we thought you'd find that in this latest group of photos. If she's not in there, then we have no idea who you're looking for," he told his employers in his most sincere tone.

Geneva stepped forward and pinned the photographer with her probing dark brown eyes. "Kent, the woman we want should personify the name of the fragrance. She should be as cool, refreshing, and captivatingly lovely as a spring breeze."

"And the two of you didn't see her in this monstrous portfolio?" Kent inquired humbly, nodding toward the book in his hands.

"Kent, those girls are all very lovely," Franklin declared, "but when Gen and I say this woman should be refreshing, we also mean she should be new. A new face, not one that's been seen in every ad from light beer to tampons. Her face will be everywhere. We want everyone who sees her to wonder who she is. We want 'em to wonder that right up until the press party the night before the fragrance hits the market. That sort of splash combined with the power shopping of the Christmas season and the New Year could mean millions."

Their meal was finished, but Casey was still berating Rencia for being such a pushover. The two friends stormed into the lobby of the restaurant, their voices and tempers raised.

"Look, give it a rest, Casey. I don't need you tellin' me how to handle my husband!"

"Ha!" Casey disagreed. "You need someone to, you let Ivan bulldoze you into doing exactly what he wants. Nothing," she whispered fiercely.

With a wave of her hand, Rencia stormed away from Casey. The small crowd from GeFran eyed them with increasing interest.

"My God," Frank Arnold breathed, his eyes focused on Rencia.

Geneva agreed with her husband. "There she is."

"Rencia!" Casey called, following her friend to the door.

"Zip it," Rencia ordered sweetly, before placing a soft kiss on Casey's cheek.

Casey sighed and watched Rencia head toward the parking lot. Then she turned and found herself looking into the faces of the four people behind her.

"Yes?" she queried, growing a bit aggravated by the group's incessant staring.

After a moment, Frank Arnold stepped forward. "We

apologize for hovering, miss, but we were wondering about your friend."

Casey watched them all suspiciously. "Why?"

Geneva Arnold pushed her husband aside and stepped before him. "I apologize for my husband, Miss . . . "

"Franklin," Casey answered after a moment's hesitation.

Geneva laughed lightly. "What a coincidence. This is my husband, *Franklin* Arnold, and I'm Geneva," she announced, shaking hands with Casey. "Ms. Franklin," she continued, "we run GeFran Cosmetics. Have you ever heard of the company?"

Casey was awestruck. "Have I ever? Yes! I use your products all the time!"

Geneva smiled. "Well, that's a compliment indeed coming from a young woman as lovely as yourself."

Casey bowed her head slightly, accepting the flattery. "So, what can I help you all with?" she asked finally.

Geneva clasped her hands together and glanced at the double glass doors near the front of the restaurant. "*Your* girlfriend who just walked out, what's her name?"

"Uh, that was my cousin Lawrencia, why?"

Geneva glanced at her associates before looking back at Casey. "We'd like to offer her a job."

Casey's mouth fell open and she was speechless for a full ten seconds. "Would you mind repeating that?"

Lawrencia eyed the crumpled newspaper with increasing disappointment. She had journeyed to the bedroom later that evening with the classified ads in hopes of finding a job she qualified for. She refused to settle for an occupation as a cashier or waitress, both of which she had experience as and knew she could do well. Unfortunately, turning away from that decision left her with few choices.

Lord, why didn't I stay in college? she asked herself. After her junior year of school, she had begged her father to pay her way for a trip to Africa. Rencia told him how she just had to go and reminded him of how educational the trip would be. Lawrence Davis, after whom she was named, couldn't argue the point and Rencia was allowed to postpone her senior year of college until the following semester.

The trip did turn out to be a wonderful experience for Rencia. It was very liberating to know she was part of a culture so rich in diversity, knowledge, and history. She and her group of eight friends visited almost every country on the continent. When they arrived in Egypt, her life was forever changed.

Ivan and his parents had been visiting the country on a pilgrimage they took once a year. Ivan and Rencia met during a tour of the Sphinx. When Ivan spotted the incredible beauty laughing and talking with her friends, he had to meet her. Rencia was just as taken by the dark gorgeous young man who kept looking her way.

It was difficult maintaining a long-distance relationship with Ivan attending college in Florida while she lived in Washington, D.C. Rencia knew she had a promise to keep to her father about school. However, she had fallen in love and college was no longer her top priority. Halfway through her first semester as a senior, she left school to be with Ivan in Florida. They lived together one year before getting married.

Now Rencia was having regrets. Not about her marriage, she loved Ivan more than anything. But she wished she'd completed her education.

"Oh well." She sighed, picking up the paper again.

"No sense harping on the past," she softly advised herself, just as the mahogany bedroom door flew open.

"What's up, Larry?" Ivan greeted in his usual manner when he used her nickname. He tossed his keys to the bureau.

"Hey, Zhabi," she called. Long ago, she'd shortened his last name, which she primarily used when they were alone. "How was your day?" she asked, shoving the newspaper aside.

Ivan laid his coat over a black armchair near the tall windows and turned his dark gaze on her. "Oh, it's shaping up," he assured her, his eyes taking a leisurely trip over Rencia's long shapely legs.

She toyed with the satin belt of her robe. "How so?" she teased.

Ivan curled his large hands around her upper arms and urged her to stand on the bed before him. She sank her fingers into his thick, dark hair just as he raised his head. Rencia moaned shamelessly as his mouth trailed over the sensitive skin of her neck. When his hands tightened around her waist, she gasped. Too soon, he was moving her to the bed, where he collapsed beside her.

Ivan's eyes narrowed when he spied the classified section of the paper on the bed. "What's that?" he asked, his soft deep voice holding just a bit of an edge.

Rencia shrugged. "The paper," she replied, as her lips stroked the strong line of his jaw.

Ivan turned his stare back to her face and simply watched her. He didn't have to wait long for her to break.

"Damn it, Zhabi, it's the want ads, all right? That's what I was looking at," she blurted.

"What for?" He moved off the bed, taking the paper with him.

Rencia gave a short laugh. "Zhabi, why do most people look at the want ads?" she questioned.

Ivan tossed the paper into the wastebasket near the bathroom door in their master suite. "*You're* looking for a job?" he asked, as though he couldn't believe it.

"I think it's about time," she stated firmly. "And I have to tell you it's not the easiest thing I've ever done. All the good jobs require a college degree or at least some type of formal training. So, on top of feeling discouraged beyond belief, I also feel incredibly stupid and irresponsible for not completing my education."

Ivan took a seat on the edge of the tangled cobalt-blue comforter. "Larry, you know you can always take the classes you need to get your degree. I support that one hundred percent."

Rencia's eyes narrowed. "You support my getting my degree, but not using that degree to get a job, right?"

Ivan stared at her again. Part of him was impressed by her determination. Another part of him was terrified by it. He pulled off the stylish salt-and-pepper jacket and tugged the matching suspenders from his broad shoulders, leaving them to dangle past his hips. Leaning against the tall bedpost, he stood watching her.

Rencia traced the stitching in the finely crafted comforter. She could almost feel Ivan's eyes shooting daggers at her.

"I don't want you working, Larry. I already told you that," he finally said, his voice low but firm.

Hating the tone of his voice, Rencia found her usually mild temper heated. "Too bad," she said after a moment.

Ivan blinked and pushed his hands into his deep pockets. "What?" he replied, watching her leave the bed.

Rencia propped her hand on her hip and cleared her throat. "I said . . . too bad."

Ivan's long sleek brows rose slightly when she repeated herself. He nodded as a cocky smirk tugged at his mouth. "What are you gonna do?" he asked. "What sort of job do you hope to find, Larry?"

Rencia's full lips tightened into a thin line. She realized he was referring to her education and limited experience. "You know, despite my disillusionment, I can do whatever I want," she informed him haughtily.

Ivan's deep rich laughter filled the spacious bedroom. He lowered his tall, athletic body to an armchair and leaned back. "Good luck," he replied.

Rencia's expression was clearly guarded. "I don't need your sarcasm, Zhabi."

Ivan chuckled. "I'm not being sarcastic, Larry," he assured her.

Rencia folded her arms across her chest and continued to regard him suspiciously. "You're not?"

"No," he confirmed, sounding honest. He enjoyed watching Rencia as she stood before him and tried to figure him out. He loved her more than his life and only wanted to take care of her.

The thought made him recall the way his father had to struggle before he'd gone into business for himself. Mikende DeZhabi's family had come to America when he was in his late teens and it paid off. After working several years in a Georgia steel plant, Mikende quit, took all his money, and began a small restaurant. Today, the Cape featured authentic West African cuisine. Establishments could be found in Atlanta, San Francisco, London, and South Africa. Anata DeZhabi, Ivan's mother, had toiled alongside her husband. Their love and faith in each other had been tested many times, but the marriage was still strong. Still, it was a struggle Ivan never wanted to put his own marriage through.

His mother's working was the reason he had grown up an only child. He remembered the day his mother announced that she was expecting another baby. Ivan spent many sleepless nights wondering if it was to be a brother or sister. The only person more excited about the new baby was his father.

However, the DeZhabis, who worked long, hard hours, didn't have much time to ponder such marvels. Anata was determined to play an equal role in the success of her family, but her strenuous routine had resulted in the loss of the expected child. The family was devastated.

Ivan had mourned the loss of the sibling he would never know. But he was more frightened by the change it brought between his parents. His father barely spoke to his mother after that and she was so devastated over the loss, Ivan wondered if she even noticed. Afterward, Mikende DeZhabi forbade his wife to ever work again. Anata was stunned by the ultimatum, but she adhered to her husband's wishes.

She didn't argue because she loved him and was committed to the survival of her marriage, Ivan thought. He remembered how it felt to have the weight of fear and uncertainty leave his young shoulders when his parents' relationship improved.

Now Rencia wanted to work. Ivan debated telling her how the situation of so long ago still affected him. Each time, he reconsidered sharing such painful memories. The fact that they were still so powerful made Ivan angry with himself for being weak. Besides, he wanted her to honor his wishes because she wanted to—not because she felt sorry for him. That he could not handle. He was sure that once she realized how difficult it would be to find a job with no experience, she would let go of the idea.

Rencia's stare was hard as she glared across the room.

"Your reverse psychology won't work, Ivan," she promised him.

The confident grin almost left Ivan's handsome face, but he maintained his composure. Sometimes, Rencia greatly unnerved him by her uncanny ability to read his motives. "That's not what I'm trying to do," he lied.

"Really?" she inquired dryly, "so what brought about this sudden decision to support me?"

Ivan pulled one hand through his twisted locks. "Damn, Larry," he groaned, "I can't win with you, can I?"

Rencia wasn't put off. "You still think I won't find anything because I have no education and no experience. That's why you figure *supporting* my decision to work won't be such a big deal."

The observation triggered the tiny muscle in Ivan's jaw. "Believe what you like, Larry," he finally told her.

Rencia sighed. "Well, thanks for your support," she said, finally deciding to drop the argument.

Chapter Two

The next morning, Rencia entered the kitchen and was greeted by the smell of hash browns and eggs. Shaking her tousled hair, she yawned and tugged on the thigh-high hemline of her nightie before walking over to the paneled counter. She watched Ivan at the table wolfing down his breakfast. Since he was a fabulous cook, she rarely had to worry about preparing their meals. She was lucky that her husband's barely concealed chauvinism didn't carry over into the kitchen duties.

"Sorry to be getting up so late," she said, filling her plate with scrambled eggs and the seasoned browns.

Ivan shrugged. "No problem," he assured her, wiping his hands on a paper towel.

Rencia set her plate on the table. Before she could sit down, Ivan pulled her over to him.

Sitting astride her husband, she wound her arms about his neck. Her fingers played in his gorgeous hair, while his hands disappeared beneath her short gown. He trailed his mouth over the smooth column of her neck. Rencia moaned as she enjoyed the double caress of his lips on her body and his hands on her thighs.

"Zhabi, don't," she resisted weakly.

Ivan's deep voice was muffled. "Why?"

"'Cause you have to go to work," she reminded him.

One of us has to, she added quietly. Standing over him, she almost gave in when his hands cupped her full bottom and gently squeezed. Ivan's sensual black eyes appraised her intently as she moved away.

"You know I can be late," he whispered, a devilish smile on his face.

Rencia chuckled and was about to walk back to him when the phone rang. "Saved by the bell," she sang, hurrying to the phone. "Rencia DeZhabi," she answered.

Casey's loud voice sounded through the line. "Hey, girl! What's up?"

"Not much, why? What's goin' on?"

"You got any plans for the day?"

Rencia rolled her eyes. "Please." She sighed. "But I may go job hunting later."

"Cancel it. Be at home around eleven," Casey ordered.

Rencia frowned. "Why, what's up?"

"Just be there, all right?"

"All right, all right, I'll be here," she promised, hanging up the phone when the connection abruptly ended.

"So when are you gonna start your job hunt?" Ivan asked when his wife returned to the table.

Rencia dug into her breakfast. "I'm not sure. I'll probably wait and start tomorrow since Casey's coming over today," she explained.

Ivan smiled at the mention of his cousin's name. *Good ol Case,* he thought, returning his attention to his plate. "Well, keep me posted if you have any luck," he urged.

Rencia watched Ivan carry his plate to the sink. After pressing a heated kiss to her mouth, he was out the door.

Rencia brushed her hands against the front of her baggy jeans as she rushed to answer the door. A frown marred her brow when she noticed that Casey had brought four people along. "Good morning, everyone, please come in," she offered with a smile. Shooting Casey a strange look, Rencia watched the group walk inside.

Once everyone was in the living room, Casey made the introductions. "Uh, Ren, this is Geneva and Franklin Arnold. They own GeFran Cosmetics."

"Mrs. DeZhabi," Frank Arnold was saying, "it's a pleasure to meet you."

Rencia shook the hand he offered. "Yes" was all she could manage.

"This is Kent Daniels and Silas Timmons," Frank continued, watching her greet the two men.

Finally, Geneva Arnold stepped forward. "Sweetie, I'm sure you're wondering what this is about?" she asked.

Rencia sighed and nodded. "Yes," she answered again, her voice filled with relief.

"May we?" Geneva asked, turning toward the sofa.

Rencia shook her head. "I'm sorry, yes, please," she said, waving them farther into the room.

"First, let me start by telling you that our newest fragrance, Breeze, is scheduled to hit the market this summer."

Rencia nodded, still confused about what was going on.

"Well," Geneva continued, "unfortunately, we haven't been able to find the right person to represent the fragrance until now. We'd like to offer you the job as spokesmodel for it."

Completely dumbstruck, Rencia let her gaze slowly slide to Casey, who was beaming. She turned back to Geneva and began to shake her head. "Mrs. Arnold—"

"Please call me Geneva. We're all very informal at GeFran," the lovely older woman explained.

Rencia nodded and cleared her throat longer than necessary.

"Geneva, I don't know about all this. I mean, I've never modeled before. You all may be making a huge mistake," she cautioned them.

"Oh, we haven't made a mistake, believe me." Geneva insisted. The founder of GeFran had decided on her Breeze Girl and her decision was final.

Silas Timmons, GeFran's marketing president, spoke up. "Mrs. DeZhabi, I know this all sounds unreal but after we explain what the job entails and what we're prepared to offer, maybe you'll feel differently. May we?"

Rencia raised her hand from the arm of the chair. "Of course," she permitted, still very uncertain, but quite intrigued.

The meeting was informative and productive. The executives from GeFran even came prepared with their proposed marketing plans for the upcoming Christmas season and beyond. As time passed, Rencia had more questions, which were all thoroughly answered.

"I'm starting to believe this is for real," she commented much later.

"It is," Frank and Kent chimed in.

"Rencia, we know all this still may be a bit overwhelming for you," Geneva guessed. "We'd like for you to think it over. Here's my card. We hope you take us up on this offer."

Rencia stood and took the card from the small woman. "Thanks," she whispered.

"Listen, Rencia, before you make any decisions, we'd like to give you a full tour of the company. Maybe it'll help you make up your mind if you view our facilities and meet the people who could be your new coworkers," Silas suggested.

Frank nodded. "Rencia, we'd like to invite you to visit our offices tomorrow morning if you're free."

Rencia was still so awestruck she didn't know what to say. Casey, however, had no problems speaking.

"Don't worry, she'll be there!" she assured them.

Everyone laughed, but Frank turned to Rencia again. "Can we get your word on that?" he requested softly.

Rencia nodded. "I'll be there."

After showing the foursome to the door, Rencia sighed and turned to Casey, who had remained in the living room.

"Ren, girl, do you know what this means?" she shrieked, clapping her hands and running in place.

Rencia's uneasiness didn't diminish. "I still can't believe it," she breathed. "Casey, you didn't set this up, did you?"

"Ren, even I couldn't think up something this good," she promised.

"Do you think I have what it takes?" Rencia asked, filled with doubt.

Casey glared at her. "I think so and, more importantly, those people at GeFran think so too."

"I wonder what Ivan'll say."

Casey snorted. "Forget my cousin, this is about you!" she ordered.

Rencia sighed and dragged her fingers through her hair. "I have to tell him, Case."

"Of course you do," Casey agreed with a shrug. "But if you want to do this, don't let him talk you out of it."

"You know, he did tell me to let him know if anything came through," she recalled.

Casey snapped her fingers. "There ya go."

Rencia sucked her teeth. "Nah . . . I don't think so. He's trying to act supportive, but I don't think he means it."

Casey expressed a knowing sigh. "Mmm . . . reverse psychology?"

"Mmm . . ." Rencia confirmed with a nod.

"Well, call his bluff."

Rencia continued to nod. That was exactly what she intended to do.

"We should probably consider doing a little something for the clients. Perhaps in the next couple of weeks."

Ivan sighed as he listened to his boss, Curtis Henderson, on the other end of the line. The man had been hinting about throwing a party for someone they hoped would become a new client of the advertising firm Cabron and McKenzie. Curtis had been talking nonstop for the past ten minutes regarding the get-together. There was no question as to who he wanted to handle it.

"Curtis, if the guy won't sign during a board meeting, he's not gonna sign at a party," Ivan said, in no mood for another client party when he'd just held one.

"That's where you're wrong. A party would most certainly cinch the deal. Especially during this time of year," Curtis argued. "They've seen some of the spreads we've done for the other big-name lingerie and cosmetics companies. As I told the powers-that-be, an informal party would almost certainly guarantee us walking away with the contract."

Ivan knew that. He'd been around long enough to know that more deals were made during dinners and small parties than anywhere else. Unfortunately, he wasn't really sold on the idea of impressing clients for a company he would soon be leaving. Still, Ivan, who was becoming increasingly shrewd as he got older, couldn't completely dismiss the idea. A party for Cabron and

McKenzie could be a golden opportunity to make even more contacts. Those contacts could turn into future clients once he and his partner, Sam Long, broke from the firm.

"All right, Curtis, you've convinced me. I suppose you want me to throw this thing?" Ivan asked, already knowing the answer.

Curtis's laughter sounded across the line. "Well, if you insist," he teased.

Ivan reclined in his chair. "Mmm . . . well, I'll call you with the details next week, sound good?"

"Sounds good," Curtis assured him before hanging up.

Ivan had just clicked off the speakerphone when it buzzed again.

"Ivan, Rencia's on the phone for you."

"Put her through," he drawled, pleased by the call. "Hey, Larry."

"Zhabi, do you think you can get away for lunch this afternoon?" Rencia asked, her voice unusually soft.

"Mmm-hmm, what's up?"

"I got somethin' I want to talk to you about."

"All right, it, um, sounds serious. You want me to come home?"

"No, no," she replied quickly, "I'd rather go out."

"Okay. We can meet at Homestyle around . . . one o'clock?"

"I'll see you there."

Ivan gently replaced the receiver and stared at the phone. Lord, how he loved that woman. More than his own life, it seemed. He often wondered if she knew that. Everything about Rencia had intrigued him from the moment he first saw her. Her beauty—definitely her beauty—her spirit, and the air of innocence and seduction that surrounded her. That combination of attributes made him want to take care of her and love her. She was his life-line and he wanted her with him always.

Lawrencia arrived at Homestyle long before one. She was glad Ivan had suggested they have lunch there. The family-owned restaurant served some of the best southern and Caribbean cuisine in town. Rencia loved the atmosphere almost as much as she enjoyed the food. It was very relaxing, and that was what she needed to be right then.

A model! She still couldn't believe those people had offered her a job like that. Though she had always received compliments on her looks, she never took any of them seriously. Many people seemed shocked when they discovered how down-to-earth she was. Of course, Rencia knew that accepting such an opportunity would produce a drastic change in her life. She would be a celebrity, not to mention financially sound. That alone was enough to make her accept the job. GeFran had laid out an impressive list of benefits that would have made anyone look twice. Rencia could only hope that when she told her husband he wouldn't hit the roof.

"Rencia, what's goin' on?"

She flinched and looked up. "Goodness, Martin, you scared me!" she cried, realizing that she was so apprehensive about talking to Ivan that she didn't notice her husband's colleague approaching the table.

Martin Godwin patted her hand as he took a seat. "I'm sorry. Is everything okay?" he asked.

"Yeah, yeah, everything's fine," she assured him. "I just had my mind on something else."

Martin smiled, gazing adoringly upon Rencia's face.

"So, what's been going on? I haven't seen you in a while."

Rencia fixed him with a bright smile and shook her head. "Not much right now, but talk to me in a few weeks and the story might be different."

Martin leaned forward. "Sounds mysterious, care to elaborate?" he asked, a slight frown tugging at his high forehead.

"I can't say just yet, but pray for me."

Martin spread his hands. "No problem," he promised with a laugh.

"Hey, Win. Man, what's up?"

Winton Charles turned to greet his friend. Ivan had just walked into the restaurant and was pulling off his coat.

"Hey, man, how's the new biz comin'?" Winton questioned.

Ivan fixed him with a frown. "Damn, it has been a long time since I've seen you. It hasn't gotten off the ground yet. We're still in the planning stages."

Winton nodded. "Well, I want a piece of the stock when this thing pops off," he demanded.

Ivan laughed and clapped Homestyle's maitre d' on the back. He turned toward the dining room. "Man, is Larry here yet?" he asked.

Winton sighed and rolled his eyes. "Hell yeah, she's here sittin' in the middle of the spot ruining my business."

Ivan looked at Winton. "How?" he asked, scratching the long, sleek line of his brow.

Winton waved his hand toward the dining room. "Hell, no one can eat for staring at her."

Ivan's deep chuckles rumbled from his chest as he looked toward the dining room. His onyx gaze finally settled on his wife and grew deadly when he spotted Martin Godwin also at the table.

Ivan, never having liked his coworker, also never liked how taken the man had always been with Rencia. With a devilish smirk crossing the curve of his mouth, he turned to Winton again. "Win, do me a favor," he said, slapping a twenty into the man's palm.

Rencia was laughing at a joke Martin had made when she saw Winton walking toward the table. "Hey, is anything wrong?" she asked him.

Winton smiled and shook his head. "No, Mrs. DeZhabi, I only wanted to let you know that Mr. DeZhabi has just arrived and is putting away his coat. Should I have the salads sent?"

Rencia sent Winton a knowing smile when he called her and Ivan by their last names, something he never did. It was easy to guess who had put him up to it, but she played along.

"That'll be fine, Winton," she assured him, faking a formal tone of voice.

Winton nodded and turned to Martin. "And, sir, will you be joining the DeZhabis for lunch?"

Martin cleared his throat. "Uh, no. No, I won't be. Rencia, I'm sorry but I do need to be getting back to the office," he explained quickly, not wanting to get on Ivan's well-known bad side.

Rencia nodded and patted his hand. "That's okay, Martin. I understand." She watched him nod before he walked away.

The moment his coworker was out of sight, Ivan arrived at the table. Rencia watched the tall, devastatingly handsome man situate himself in his seat and she shook her head at him.

"Why do you always treat Martin that way?" she asked, playfully.

Ivan tugged the stylish mocha tie away from his neck and shrugged. "He likes you too much" was his soft reply, before he took a large gulp from his glass of milk. "What'd you want to talk about?"

Rencia's long lashes closed over her eyes as she took a deep breath. "I've been offered a job," she blurted.

Ivan's eyes narrowed and he appeared to choke a bit on his milk. "Who would hire you?" he inquired bluntly. At the hurt expression on her face, he rephrased the question. "I'm sorry, Larry, who offered you a job?"

Rencia shifted in her seat. "Have you ever heard of GeFran Cosmetics?"

Intrigued, Ivan nodded. "The firm's done some layouts for them," he said, referring to Cabron and McKenzie.

"Well, that's who offered me the job."

"Doing what?" he asked, propping the side of his face against his palm.

Rencia ran both hands though her thick hair and leaned forward. "Frank and Geneva Arnold, the company's owners, told me about this new fragrance they'll be marketing soon. They want me to represent it. They want me to be the spokesmodel for the product," she announced.

Ivan ignored the aggravating pain in his chest, still not believing what he was hearing. "How'd they find out about you?"

"Yesterday they saw me in the Shellfish with Casey and they asked about me and . . . that was that," she answered, not liking the look on his face.

After a moment, he shrugged. "Well, it would've been nice," he mumbled, taking another sip of his milk.

"It would've been nice? What the hell is that supposed to mean?" Rencia snapped.

"Baby, you can't be taking this seriously," he stated, his disbelief clear.

"What if I am?" she challenged.

"Forget it," he said cooly, focusing on his glass.

Rencia's mouth fell open and she leaned back in her chair. "What happened to all this support crap you were talking this morning?" she whispered.

Ivan shrugged one massive shoulder. "You won't take that job, Larry," he assured her. "While the Arnolds were dazzling you with their offer, they should have bothered to tell you how unstable modeling is."

Rencia leaned back in her chair and fiddled with the wide collar of her lime-green silk blouse. "The Arnolds didn't have to tell me that, because I already knew that."

"Well then, why the hell are you so interested in it? I would rather have you working for Maurice Stiles Catering than doing this."

"*You* would rather?" she said, anger spewing from her emerald gaze. "Zhabi, when will you start to understand that this has nothing to do with you? For once, I'm doing something that's all about me."

Ivan massaged his jaw. "But modeling, Larry?"

"Oh, baby, please. I have no fantasies about this," she assured him, reaching across the table to pull his hand between both of hers. "If you must know, it's the money and sense of accomplishment, not the possibility of fame, clothes, or adoration, that I'm interested in. I'm also very determined to finish my degree, and when I decide to go back to school, this job would allow me to pay for it."

Ivan's uncommonly long lashes fluttered as a smile creased his face. "Larry, if that's why you need the money, I could—"

"No, Zhabi, this is something I have to do, I want to do for myself."

"Well, if it would make you feel better, you could pay me back," he teased, watching his wife fix him with a look that removed the grin from his face. "I'm done with this, Larry. I don't like the idea of you working and I won't change my opinion of that."

Rencia was so angry her hands shook. "One minute you're supporting me and the next you're telling me to forget the whole thing. Tell me, does being such a liar ever bother you, Zhabi?" she yelled, stabbing the table with her fork.

Ivan's rock-hard stare snapped to his face before he lowered his glass. He pointed a finger in her direction. "You don't want to argue with me about this, so I suggest you drop it." His soft voice was laced with ice.

Rencia slapped at his extended finger. She was seconds away from dashing the rest of the milk into his gorgeous face when they were interrupted.

"Ivan, Rencia, I didn't know you two would be here! Boy, it's getting cold out there."

The couple retreated to their mutual corners as Curtis Henderson took a seat at the table. Rencia turned to her husband's boss and gave him a lovely yet phony smile. "Good to see you, Curtis," she said.

Curtis patted her hand. "It's good to see you too, my dear. Say, did Ivan tell you about the party I spoke with him about giving?"

Rencia turned a cold stare toward Ivan and grimaced. "Another party? No, he didn't mention it."

Curtis sensed the tension in the air. "I'm sorry . . . did I interrupt something?" he asked.

Suddenly, Rencia could stand no more of Ivan just staring at her. Angrier than she had ever been, she stood from the table. Her eyes never left her husband's face as she spoke to Curtis. "I'm sorry, Curtis, but I stopped eating swine a long time ago and I'm not about to have lunch with this one." She tossed her fork to the table and walked away with the grace of a queen.

Curtis's eyes widened and he watched Rencia bolt away. He turned back to Ivan and his mouth formed a perfect O as he watched the brooding younger man bend his knife in half.

When Ivan arrived home much later that evening, he found Rencia asleep in his favorite chair. She was still dressed in the stylish pantsuit she'd worn to lunch. Ivan figured she must have fallen asleep right after she'd gotten home. A smile softened his striking features as he watched her. He never expected things to turn out the way they had.

Her news that afternoon had shocked him to his soul, and that was probably even an understatement. Wincing, he remembered how it felt to hear her call him a liar. He kept forgetting that she could read him so well. He should never have tried to hide his true feelings from her, but he never thought she would have any luck. He knew she was smart enough to do anything she wanted, but she'd never seemed to want for anything until now. Plus, having her waiting for him when he got home was just the way he liked it. Chauvanistic perhaps, but he had his reasons.

Turning away from the comfortable living room, he

headed upstairs and prepared to take a shower. The
water coursing over the chiseled muscles of his body
cleared his mind a bit. Sadly, Ivan held on to the idea
that if he stood firm about Rencia not taking the job, she
would soon forget it.

Rencia woke with a jerk and immediately groaned, realizing that she had a bad cramp in her neck. After
having driven around for hours trying to calm herself,
she had finally come home and dropped into the first
chair she saw.

Pushing herself out of the seat, she headed upstairs.
By the time she entered the master bedroom suite, she
had stripped down to her underthings. Piling her thick
hair atop her head and securing it with a pin, she
stepped into the bathroom adjoined to the bedroom.

When she heard the shower running, her first impulse
was to use the guest bathroom. However, something
stopped her. The run-in with Ivan earlier had brought
something out in her. Standing up to him, really standing up to him, made her feel something she hadn't felt
in so long. Rencia loved her husband with everything
in her, but the time for being submissive was wearing
thin.

Rencia was busy brushing her teeth when Ivan turned
off the shower and opened the sliding glass doors. As he
stood rubbing the thick black bath sheet across his body,
his eyes roamed over her body with raw desire. She could
almost feel him stripping away the lacy peach bra and
matching boy shorts she wore. Unfortunately, she was in
no mood to be admired.

Ivan wrapped the towel around his hips and stepped
from the shower. Before he could reach her, Rencia

moved away from the sink and went to hold open the bathroom door. A smirk tugged at Ivan's mouth and he took the hint to leave. Rencia slammed the door shut and began running water in the tub.

After relaxing in the steamy bubble bath for almost an hour, Rencia toweled off and lotioned in the bathroom. When she stepped into the darkened bedroom, she used the light from the bathroom to find her way. It didn't take long to locate a cream silk nightie to slip into.

Looking forward to a comfortable night's sleep, she quickly slipped between the crisp black cotton sheets. No sooner had she gotten settled than a hand curled around her arm and she was pulled to the other side of the bed.

Ivan didn't say a word, but his hands and mouth were everywhere. Strong fingers tugged the straps of Rencia's gown from her slender shoulders as his mouth trailed the line of her neck and his heavenly lips pressed teasing wet kisses to the heavy globes on her chest.

Rencia's lashes fluttered open and closed as Ivan tugged mercilessly at her stiffening peaks. Oblivious to everything except his touch, she let her long legs shift apart and she pulled his hand from her chest to her thigh. Ivan was happy to fulfill the unspoken request to caress the tight heat there. His mouth continued to work feverishly over her ample breasts. Deep groans matched her soft cries perfectly. The pleasure was almost impossible to resist, but somehow she found the will to do just that.

"Ivan . . . Ivan, stop . . . Ivan?"

"What?" he groaned, his mouth teasing the satiny skin beneath her breasts.

"Stop," she repeated, pressing her hands against his massive chest. In response, she heard him chuckle and she strained against him again.

Ivan took notice then. Even in the dark, his eyes were

penetrating. "Why are you pushing me away?" he asked, sounding wounded.

Rencia began to squirm away from him. "You know why."

Ivan pushed his thick hair from his face and leaned closer. "Tell me."

"Hello in there," she sang, knocking against his forehead. "Did you forget our lunch date today? Do you really think we should have sex after that?"

Ivan's hand slid up the smooth line of her thigh. "This has nothin' to do with that," he reasoned, lowering his mouth to a pouting nipple.

"The hell you say!" she argued, holding him off with both hands.

Aggravated and aroused, Ivan slammed one fist into his pillow. "Do you know how frustrating this is?"

"Good. Now you know how I've felt all damn day."

"What the hell has gotten into you?"

Rencia laughed. "Some sense. Sense has finally gotten into me. Thank goodness!"

"Rencia—"

"You know what, Zhabi? I don't even want to talk about this anymore. So just forget it. Forget the whole thing!"

"What are you saying?"

"It's not worth it to go through all this with you. Good night!"

Ivan watched his wife move over to the other side of the bed. He shrugged and smiled, figuring she wasn't willing to go through with the job if it meant dealing with his objection. Little did he know that Rencia had other ideas.

Chapter Three

The alarm clock sounded very early the next morning. As usual, Ivan was first to get up. Rencia almost always got up with him and they would eat breakfast together before he headed off to work. That morning, however, was different. When Ivan left the bathroom after his shower, he saw that Rencia was still in bed. A slight frown tugged at his sleek brows as he watched his wife sprawled across the covers, her long hair covering her face. He tried not to let it bother him and started to dress. His onyx gaze was repeatedly drawn to the bed. His stare grew stormier by the moment.

Rencia felt herself being shaken awake some time later. Her eyes opened just enough to see Ivan's handsome face looming above her. With a yawn, she tried to turn back over.

"Larry?" he called, his grip firming.

"Hmm?" was her relaxed response.

Ivan's mouth tensed into a thin line as he grimaced. "I'm leaving."

Rencia wriggled her fingers and gave him a sleepy smile. "Bye," she whispered, snuggling deeper into the covers.

Ivan let go of her arm and bolted away from the bed. The door slammed viciously behind him.

* * *

"Hey, girl, it's me!"

Rencia smiled as Casey's boisterous voice came through the phone line. "What's up, hon?"

"I should be asking you that. Are you goin' on that tour today?"

Knowing that Casey was referring to her scheduled tour of GeFran Cosmetics, Rencia nodded. "Mmm-hmm, I'm getting ready right now."

"Good for you! So what'd Ivy say when you told him?" Casey asked, an expectant tone coloring her words.

Rencia replaced her perfume bottle on the dresser. "Case, it was a mess. Your cousin acted the fool. I thought if we talked out in public, it might've gone better."

"Honey, you know Ivy don't care about appearances," Casey reminded her friend.

Rencia sighed. "I know, but I was desperate. I just couldn't believe he'd lie to me like that, just outright lie! Pretending to support me like that."

"I'm sorry, girl," Casey soothed. "I still can't believe you're goin' through with it though."

Rencia sighed again and ran a brush through her hair. "It's an opportunity, Casey. An opportunity that I'd like to take advantage of."

Casey laughed. "Well, you go on, girl!" Her overly enthusiastic response drew laughter from Rencia. "So, um, what are you gonna tell Ivan?"

"Nothing."

"Excuse me?"

"You heard me."

Casey was silent for a moment. "You're sure about this?"

"What the hell for, Case? So he can lie to me again,

or better yet, so he can act like a caveman again? Telling me no, and that's final? Uh-uh, no way. I've gotta stop trying to please him all the time. Especially if it's at the expense of my own happiness."

"Sounds good, sista. I hope you know what you're doing." Casey's voice was filled with caution, but she was pleased by her friend's determination.

Rencia smiled at herself in the mirror. "Oh, I know what I'm doing," she assured Casey, praying to herself that she did.

"Rencia! So glad you could make it!"

Rencia shook hands with Frank Arnold and hugged Geneva. She had just walked into the cooly elegant lobby of GeFran Cosmetics. The main office was located in Manhattan and it far exceeded anything she could have imagined.

"Do you have any questions before we get started?" Geneva asked.

Rencia shook her head. "Not yet, but by the time we get halfway through the tour, I'll probably have about a million," she warned the tiny woman.

Frank stepped forward and offered one arm to his wife and the other to Rencia. "Well, first, we're going to stop in the dining room for breakfast. Rencia, you haven't eaten yet, have you?"

"Only a bowl of cereal."

Frank nodded. "Well, young lady, you're in for a real treat. This way," he directed.

The tour was a complete success. Everyone who met Lawrencia DeZhabi congratulated the Arnolds on making such a perfect choice. Rencia's poise and beauty, not to mention her sweet personality, were a hit with all GeFran employees.

Aside from the people, the building itself was just as impressive. Class, sophistication, money, and influence were just a few words that could be used to describe the place. By the end of the tour, Rencia found herself regretting that it was over. Soon, the Arnolds were showing her back to the executive offices on the thirtieth floor.

"Well, Lawrencia, what do you think?" Geneva asked expectantly, clasping her small hands together.

"Well, they say if something seems too good to be true, then it probably is. I can't help but think that way about this. I hope you can understand that."

"We understand perfectly, dear," Geneva assured her. "This would be quite overwhelming for anyone."

"And what we have in store for this campaign would surely overwhelm the most seasoned professional," Frank chimed in.

"And what exactly do you all have in store for this campaign?" Rencia asked.

"Does this mean you're interested?"

Rencia rubbed her hands together and fixed Geneva with a knowing look. "I'm confident that I could successfully promote this product."

The soft declaration brought laughter to the office. Frank and Geneva jumped from their seats and hurried forward to shake her hand.

"This is simply wonderful!" Geneva cried. Her round chocolate face appeared more radiant than usual.

"My dear, your life is about to change in ways you've never imagined!"

Rencia was almost dizzy from all the excitement surrounding her. "You two are gonna make it hard for me to keep my feet on the ground."

Franklin laughed louder and pulled Rencia close. "Sweetheart, believe me, it'll be some time before your feet touch the ground again."

"Well, how long are you guys gonna keep me in suspense?" she inquired, slapping her hands to her thighs.

Geneva regained her composure and took Rencia's elbow in a light grasp. "Let's have a seat," she instructed, nodding toward her husband when they were all comfortable.

"The Breeze campaign promises to be our most ambitious endeavor yet," Frank began, his dark eyes gleaming with anticipation. "As we mentioned before, Breeze marks our debut in the fragrance industry. Therefore, we intend to make a spectacular splash. The young woman representing the scent will be no less spectacular," he added, flamboyantly motioning toward Rencia. "Her face will be everywhere: magazines, newspapers, billboards, even TV."

"TV?" Rencia parroted.

"Of course. We can't eliminate our most powerful medium, especially during the Christmas season, which is right around the corner."

"That's right, Lawrencia," Geneva concurred. "In addition to advertising, there will be tons of publicity tours and press conferences."

"Goodness," Rencia breathed, "I had no idea. I pray I don't disappoint you all."

"Never," Frank vowed. "We understand that you're new to this. Everyone you will come in contact with will understand that as well. We want to make this an enjoyable experience for everyone involved."

"And, Rencia, we'd like everyone to include Ivan."

Rencia's lashes shielded her gaze. "Hmph. Good luck."

"Is it that bad?" Geneva asked.

"You have no idea."

"So he's completely against you doing this?"

"Completely, Frank."

Geneva sat tapping one round French-tipped nail to her chin. "There must be something we can do to get him to feel more positive about this," she said.

"Hmph, there is, dump me and find another girl," Rencia suggested sourly.

"Now, you shouldn't get yourself upset about this," Frank interjected. "I can understand Ivan's concern. His beautiful wife is about to be thrust into a world of considerable glamour, fame, and notoriety. He probably feels he's going to lose you or some part of you."

"Oh, Frank, Ivan isn't going to lose me," Rencia assured her new boss, even as the light dimmed in her green eyes. "But this mood of his," she breathed.

"I've got it!" Geneva cried suddenly, clapping her hands together. "We'll have a party. Nothing big and splashy, just a little get-together of our executive staff and advertising team. Something to introduce the newest member of the GeFran family."

"Say, Gen, that's not a bad idea," Frank returned. "Ivan can meet the people his wife will be working for and see that we're not such monsters. Plus, our advertising team will be on hand and that's his area of expertise, right, Lawrencia?"

"I don't think a party's such a good idea."

Geneva sat a bit straighter. "Why ever not, child?"

"Because I haven't exactly told him that I'm going to do this. Ivan is under the impression that I've given up the notion."

"Ah . . ." Frank sighed. "Well, this may be your perfect opportunity to talk about your working again."

Rencia **groan**ed and massaged the dull ache forming near her **temple**s. "It's not that simple with Ivan."

Geneva **cleared her** throat and motioned for Frank to make him**self sca**rce. Once the door was closed behind her husb**and, she** took a closer seat next to Rencia.

"Sweetie**, is** Ivan only against your being a model or is he against the idea of you working in any capacity?"

"I don't really know, Geneva. I mean, I had somewhat of an opportunity with a client of his and he seemed as though he would've preferred my doing that instead of this."

"Then perhaps there's hope after all."

"Huh?"

Geneva stood. "Well, it's probably just as my husband said. Ivan's concerned that we want to change you, to take you away from him somehow. I believe he'll feel better about all this once he meets us."

Rencia's arched brows rose a bit higher. "You really believe that?"

"Well, sweetie, he's got to be told, and a party just might cushion the blow. You have to decide if you're ready for all the obstacles and difficulties this may create. Do you want this badly enough?"

Did she want it badly enough? Rencia replayed the phrase silently in her mind. The chance to be on her own? Financial independence, something she'd never known. To call her own shots, to work hard and see the results of that hard work?

"Oh yes, Geneva," she said, allowing her smile to shine through. "I definitely want this badly enough."

* * *

"So when do you think we'll be ready?" Sam Long asked.

Ivan sighed and tapped his fingers on his desk. "I figure in about three months. No less than that."

Sam and Ivan had been close friends for about five years. When they both came to work for Cabron and McKenzie, they knew they would be in business together someday.

"So what are you gonna do about this party Curt wants you to throw?" Sam asked.

"Throw it."

"Get the hell out. What for, if we're leaving?"

"Man, that's it right there. Do you know how many more contacts we could make at a party like that?"

Sam ran his hand over his shaved head and considered Ivan's outlook. "You got a point there. So is Rencia prepared for another big throw-down?"

"Man . . ." Ivan sighed, with a weary shake of his head.

Sam frowned and leaned forward in his chair. "What's goin' on?"

Ivan debated for a moment, then decided to confide in his friend. "She wants to work."

Sam stared blankly. "And?"

Ivan sent him an evil dark look. "That's it."

"So what?"

"So, I don't want her to."

Sam grinned. "You know how you sound, right?"

Ivan only shrugged a shoulder. "I don't care how I sound. I don't want her to do it," he insisted softly.

Sam nodded, appreciating his friend's honesty. "You're being very unfair about this, man. Hell, any brotha with a wife who looked like Rencia would want her to be there waiting for him when he got home. But if working is what's gonna make her happy, then, man, you'd be a fool to try and stop her."

Ivan rolled his dark eyes at Sam. "Thank you, Montell," he replied sarcastically.

Sam pressed a hand to his chest. "Man, arrogance and stubborness can ruin a marriage. Trust me, I know."

Ivan nodded, knowing Sam was speaking the truth. He had been through a messy divorce that had almost been his undoing.

Ivan, however, was confident that things would never get that far with him and Rencia. Besides, he was certain that she would soon get over her ridiculous notions about modeling, or working at all for that matter. He had reached her on her car phone and asked her to meet him at the office that day. He hoped she'd had time to come to her senses.

Ivan's phone interrupted his conversation with Sam a short while later. He leaned across the desk to answer. "Yeah, Cat?"

"Ivan, if you and Sam are done in there, Rencia's here to see you," the assistant announced.

A confident smirk brightened Ivan's face. "Yeah, Cat, tell her to come on in."

"Remember what I said, man," Sam chimed in, watching the confidence leave his friend's face.

Rencia walked into the office then. The happiness and self-assurance surrounding her were very hard to miss. So hard, in fact, that Ivan wasn't sure what to expect from his wife at that point. He sat quitely behind his desk and waited.

Rencia noticed the meek, little boy expression on her husband's handsome face. He was perfectly still with both hands lying flat on his desk, his eyes following her every move.

"What's got you lookin' so happy? Santa already visited?"

Rencia looked over at Sam and smiled. "Just because you always look evil as hell doesn't mean the rest of us can't be happy," she teased as they embraced each other.

Sam bawked, holding his hand high in the air. "Yeah, whateva! So are you really as happy as you look?"

Rencia sent him a serene smile and nodded. "Happier," she assured him, though her warm smile faded when she glanced Ivan's way. "You wanted to see me?"

Ivan blinked a couple of times in response to the firmness of her words. "Uh . . . yeah, I needed to talk to you."

Rencia extended her hands. "Well? What about? I don't have all day."

Sam Long's mouth fell open and Ivan tilted his head to the side as he stared at his wife.

"We're gonna throw a party in a few weeks," Ivan informed her as he rocked back and forth in his chair.

Rencia nodded and stepped closer to the desk. "*We* are? You're gonna help me?"

"I won't have time."

"So, what you meant to say was I would be throwing a party?" she clarified, watching Ivan shrug. "I assume this is the party Curtis was talking about the other day?"

"His wife, Kendra, offered to help out," Ivan shared. "She told me to tell you she'd be over early in the morning."

Rencia pulled a piece of lint from her stylish cashmere jacket. "I can't meet her in the morning. I have an appointment. I'll give her a call," she decided, just as her cell phone rang.

Sam watched Rencia for a long moment before turning to Ivan. Ivan's long sleek brows were drawn together and his darkly handsome face was a picture of confusion.

"Who is that?" Sam whispered to Ivan, pointing toward the door.

Ivan ran a hand through his thick locks. "I was just about to ask you."

Rencia wrapped up her call a few moments after Sam left the office.

"You seem hurried," Ivan noted.

"I am," she confirmed, flopping down into one of the charcoal-gray armchairs before his desk. "I've got a lot going on and I'd like to discuss it with you."

Ivan fought to keep the suspicion from his dark eyes and decided to busy himself looking through folders. "Start talking. I'm all ears."

Thankful for the papers distracting his gaze, Rencia finally allowed her unease to show. "I wanted to invite you to a party."

"For who?"

"For me."

Ivan's hands stilled on his desk and he smiled. "Have I forgotten a date?"

"A date?"

"It's not your birthday," Ivan muttered, certain he had forgotten some special ocassion. "And our anniversary is still a ways off."

"No, Zhabi, no. It's not that type of party."

Ivan reclined in the huge swivel chair. "I'm confused."

"I decided to take the job with GeFran Cosmetics. The Arnolds want to give a small party announcing my decision to join their company and I'd like you to be there."

Ivan massaged his jaw in an attempt to appear calm. "I thought you were going to forget about it."

Rencia let her heavy curls fall forward to partially shield her face. "I'm sorry you thought that."

"So you went on and made the decision without talking to me about it?"

"Why come to you again when I already knew how you felt about it?"

"And knowing how I felt, you chose to do it anyway?"

"Ivan, you are not my father. Lawrence Davis lives in Washington, D.C., remember?"

Ivan remained seated. "I'm not trying to be your father, Larry. But this is a very unstable career choice you're making here," he cautioned.

"Listen to you," she cried, on the verge of laughter. "What do you even know about this career choice?"

"I know that if you decide to do this, you'll hardly have time to sleep or eat or spend time with your friends. Or me."

Rencia pulled her bottom lip between her teeth and favored her husband with a soft stare. "So that's it?" she queried, easing out of the chair to saunter around behind the desk. "Baby, this could be very good for us, you know?"

"You've lost me," Ivan replied, resting his head back against the chair as he watched his wife.

Rencia perched against the desk and folded her arms across the black linen coatdress she wore. "Well, for one thing, our dinner conversations won't be so one-sided."

"Larry, I—"

"Now, wait a minute, just let me say this," she urged. "Zhabi, finally I'll get to feel like I'm doing something that really matters. Something I'll really want to share with you."

Ivan's expression hardened. "And you don't feel that you're doing that now?"

Rencia knew what he meant. "Baby, I love you. I love us—our relationship, our marriage. But, sweetie, this is something I've never had. The satisfaction that only comes from having a career, a purpose. I want that and I intend to have it."

Ivan appeared entranced as he stared into her exotic eyes. He toyed with a lock of her brown hair, before pressing it to his mouth.

"All I want is for you to meet Frank and Geneva," Rencia whispered, smoothing her hands across Ivan's hard thighs outlined beneath his dark tweed trousers. "I believe you'll feel a lot better about this once you see how great they are, how stable their company is."

"Hmph." Ivan gestured with a slow shake of his head. "Come here," he whispered, curving his hand around her neck as he drew her close.

"Mmm, does this mean yes?" Rencia asked, shivering beneath the slow wet kisses.

In one quick motion, Ivan hoisted her svelte frame across his lap. "I think I need a little more convincing."

"An introduction party?"

"That's right, and we want you and all the other models there as a show of support and welcome." Geneva rolled her eyes and grimaced toward the striking vanilla-complexioned beauty pacing the office. "

"That's funny. I don't recall having an introduction party. I don't recall having one of those when I joined your little organization."

Hester, this young woman has no experience and we want to do everything we can to set her at ease."

"She has no experience and you all are entrusting her to handle a campaign of this magnitude?"

"She has everything we're looking for."

Hester Morgan was seething inside. Her wide, midnight eyes held a fierceness that could set the strongest person on edge. "Maybe no one else has the guts to say this, Geneva, but I know all the models are thinking it."

Geneva stiffened and recrossed her legs. "And what are all the models thinking?"

"That one of us should have been chosen to represent this fragrance."

"Hester—"

"Please don't tell me I'm being unfair here, Geneva. The opportunity to be the face of Breeze? A fragrance with a New Year's debut and everything that entails? It could skyrocket any career."

"Any career, Hester? Or just yours?"

Hester's eyes narrowed and she propped one hand on her hip. "My career's just fine, Geneva, due in no small part to the fact that my contract with GeFran is almost up. It's given me the opportunity to consider many new jobs."

Geneva managed a small smile. "And I'll take that comment as assurance you won't be renewing your contract with us?"

"I may have considered it once, but after this . . . I really couldn't say."

"Very haughty, aren't we?"

Hester tilted back her head. "I think I've earned it."

Geneva's gaze was unusually frigid as she watched the slender young woman saunter around in a skintight crimson cotton dress. "You earned it because we gave you the opportunity to earn it. Remember, Ms. Morgan, you yourself only had moderate success before coming to work here. With the exception of four or five names, I can't think of any other highly regarded or highly paid black models. We not only hire our models for ads, we offer them lucrative contracts, which means steady work, Hester. Now, even though we have our own team of in-house models, we still have to venture out every once in a while to add more players to that team. We have a new fragrance, a new way we want to promote this, and we'd like a new face to go along with it. As a model who was once struggling and in need of a break herself, I should think you could easily applaude this."

"All right, all right," Hester whispered, fingering her short, curly crop of hair. "You've made your point."

"Have I?" Geneva retorted, as she inspected one of the diamonds decorating her left hand. "I suppose I won't know that until I see your smiling face at our little party on Saturday night."

Hester seemed to cringe as she spoke. "I'll be there with bells on."

"*Gentlemen's Corner* magazine just got an advertising contract from Delicious Delicates Lingerie. Since we handle advertising for DDL, that opens up a whole new avenue for us."

"Good work, Martin," commended Russel White, Cabron and McKenzie's advertising manager. "Do you have any ideas for the spreads yet?"

Martin Godwin's smile reflected pure mischief. "Well, Russ, it is *Gentlemen's Corner.* I'll be meeting with them in person next week, but I've already gotten the word that they want these ads as hot as hot can be."

"And comin' from *Gentlemen's Corner*, that ain't surprisin'," Sam Long playfully acknowledged, followed by a round of laughter from his colleagues.

"Well, Martin, keep us posted on the campaign and let me know if you need any extra brains on this."

"Thanks, Russ, you'll be the first to know."

"And if that's everything," Russ said, rubbing his

hands together, "I'll see you guys on Monday. Have a good weekend."

Sam gathered his powerbook and other accessories. He glanced toward Ivan, who had yet to move from his spot at the long conference table.

"What's up, man? You hardly said two words . . . Ivan?"

"Hmm? Oh yeah, I'm comin'."

"Ivan," Sam called, motioning for his friend to remain seated. "What the hell is wrong with you, man?"

Ivan rested his forehead on the polished cherry-wood conference table and groaned. "Rencia's draggin' me to this damned GeFran party on Saturday night."

"Ah . . . goin' to meet the new bosses?" Sam guessed.

Ivan sat up and rolled his eyes. "I just don't know about this, man."

"What? Look, it's a party. Just go there and try to have a good time. If not for yourself, do it for Ren."

Ivan fixed Sam with a stern glare. "Damn you," he muttered.

"Anytime," Sam replied, glee written all across his handsome features.

Chapter Four

Rencia turned to Ivan as he parked the 4Runner along the horseshoe driveway outside Frank and Geneva Arnold's Long Island estate. The white lights lining the rooftop and white columns along the long porch boasted of the coming holiday season.

"Baby, thank you. I know you didn't want to come, but—"

"Hey," Ivan whispered, brushing his thumb across her mouth, "it's a party, right? I just want to have a good time with you. It's been a while since we've done that."

"You're so right," she agreed, pressing her forehead against his. "This is gonna be a lot of fun and I promise you'll love Frank and Geneva."

Ivan forced a smile to brighten his features. He leaned forward to plant a lingering kiss to his wife's lips. Then he patted her thigh. "Let's get in there, then."

Upon entering, Rencia was pleased to see GeFran's marketing president rushing toward her. She clutched Ivan's arm and they headed across the spacious cream-and-gold-checkered foyer.

"I'm so glad to see you," she breathed, before turning

to Ivan. "Silas Timmons, this is my husband, Ivan DeZhabi. Ivan, Silas is GeFran's marketing president."

"Ivan, it's good to meet you," Silas greeted, as he extended his hand. "Your wife is a wonderful lady."

"Yes, she is," Ivan agreed as he shook hands with the man. "I only hope I get to keep seeing her once she starts working for you guys," he teased.

"Well, she will definitely be a busy lady," Silas warned, "but we'll never forget that she's also a married lady. Unlike most of us, she has a life!"

Rencia rested her hand against Silas's arm. "Thanks for telling him that. I believe my husband is afraid that one day I'll leave the house and never come back."

Ivan bristled beneath the comment. Thankfully, neither Silas nor Rencia seemed to notice.

"So, Ivan, what business are you in?" Silas asked, once the laughter had settled.

Ivan had just accepted a drink from a passing waiter. "Advertising," he replied.

Silas smoothed one hand across the back of his faded cut. "Advertising? Are you on your own or with an agency?"

A tiny smile played around Ivan's mouth as he spoke. "Right now, I'm with Cabron and McKenzie."

"Cabron and McKenzie . . ." Silas breathed, recognition dawning in his walnut-brown eyes. "They've handled a lot of spots for us."

"Effective ones, I hope?" Ivan inquired, chuckling when Silas raised one hand in the air.

"They were all incredibly effective. You know, Ivan, we have an in-house team, but we're gonna be in the market for an outside agency to handle the bulk of the promotions for our new Breeze fragrance."

Ivan's eyes narrowed. "Is that right?"

"I've got that tidbit directly from advertising and I wouldn't be above putting in a good word for you."

Ivan's grin triggered the striking dimples embedded at the corners of his mouth. "Well then, we should definitely talk."

Silas reached into the inside pocket of his silver-gray suit jacket and extracted a card. "Give me a call on Monday. I'll get you a meeting with Pammy Michaels, she's my VP of marketing and the one handling the campaign."

Rencia beamed as she watched Silas and Ivan wrap up their conversation. "See? Now tell me you're sorry you came to this thing," she gloated, folding her arms across the backless ankle-length cream evening gown that gloved her curvy frame.

Ivan patted his hand against the lapel of his black suit coat and shrugged. "No comment." He pulled his wife close. "So, is there any dancing goin' on in this place?"

Rencia snuggled closer and trailed the rounded tip of a petal-pink index nail along the sensuous curve of his mouth. "Why don't we go find out?" she suggested, taking his upper arm in both her hands.

All eyes followed the stunning couple as they strolled into the spacious room of influential guests. The DeZhabis, however, were oblivious to the crowd as they swayed next to the thirteen foot Christmas tree decorating the ballroom. Rencia smoothed her fingers over and under the lapels of Ivan's coat before easing her arms around his neck. A slow smile touched her mouth as she sank her fingers into his gorgeous midnight twists. Ivan's deep-set gaze was frighteningly intense as he caressed his wife's oval face.

* * *

"So, that's the million-dollar girl, hmm?"

Kathy McGee's fake blue eyes twinkled with mischief. "Nah, Hes, I think she's more like the fifty-million-dollar girl."

Hester's gaze was riveted on the fiercely beautiful couple swaying against the jazzy holiday tunes filling the air. "Good Lord," she breathed, when she took a longer look at Ivan.

Kathy's smile was knowing. "My sentiments exactly."

"Don't tell me that's her husband?" Hester remarked, as she watched the gorgeous giant who whisked Lawrencia DeZhabi around the dance floor.

"That is most certainly her husband," Kathy confirmed, trailing her nails against her ample cleavage. "With a man like that, I'd never want to leave the house."

"Hell, forget leaving the house, I'd never leave the bed!" Hester whispered, her husky laughter rising as she toyed with the necklace she wore.

"Hmph," Kathy grunted while shaking her head, "just like that, this girl has a multimillion-dollar job, she's about to be famous beyond her wildest dreams, and on top of all that, her husband is a god. There's no denying she's a lucky woman."

"Mmm, she's too lucky," Hester added. The smile curling her lips mirrored the evil intentions filling her mind.

"Frank and Geneva Arnold, this is my husband, Ivan DeZhabi."

Frank Arnold stepped forward with an outstretched hand. "Pleasure to meet you, man."

"Same here, Mr. Arnold," Ivan replied, covering Frank's hand with his own as they shook.

"Ivan, please, it's Frank and Geneva. We're not formal

around here," Geneva said as she rested one hand along Ivan's forearm.

"I think I can handle that." He flashed the lovely older woman his dimpled grin.

"Good," Geneva whispered as she clasped her small hands together. "Why don't we all find a quieter place to talk?"

"This way, Ivan," Frank called, clapping the younger man's shoulder as they walked on ahead.

Geneva slipped her hand through the crook of Rencia's arm. "Now I understand."

Rencia's long arched brows drew closed. "You understand what?"

Geneva shrugged as she stared straight ahead. "Ivan is quite magnificent to look at. I'm sure he's just as magnificent in other ways."

"Geneva!"

"What, dear?" Geneva cried as she chuckled. "I'm not that old, you know? I'm sure he keeps you very busy. I can certainly understand how difficult it must be to decide on having your time occupied by something that takes you away from him."

Rencia tossed her head back, sending a wild array of brown curls across her shoulders. "I think I can handle it."

"Mmm-hmm." Geneva sighed, leaning closer. "You can handle it, but can he?"

"So, Ivan, Lawrencia tell us that you feel she's stepping into an unstable business," Frank said.

Ivan glanced up at his wife, who was perched on the arm of the black overstuffed chair he occupied. "Well, in advertising, you see a lot of sides to the modeling business that aren't too flattering."

"We fully agree," Geneva said and exchanged nods with Frank. "Which is why we take great care in planning the contracts we offer our models."

Ivan trailed his fingers beneath the split in Rencia's gown. "What sort of planning?"

"Well, our package for Rencia would be wholly centered on the Breeze fragrance," Frank explained. "We have a slew of photo sessions scheduled. These shots will appear in magazines as well as billboards. Once the buzz is out about her, the press conferences will begin."

"That's right, Ivan," Geneva piped in. "Everyone's going to want to know who Rencia is. Where she came from. They're going to want a lot of her, and that means increased exposure."

"And that means more photo shoots," Frank agreed. "Then there will be commercials, promotional tours, and many other exciting things."

As Frank and Geneva discussed the plans for their newest "face," Rencia smiled. The Arnolds were successfully breaking down Ivan's arguments that modeling could not be a stable profession. She could barely hide her pleasure over their words. Ivan's hand tightened on her thigh just then and she looked down. Nothing prepared her for the set look she saw on his face. Of course, the Arnolds would think he was just concentrating on what they were saying, but Rencia knew differently.

Ivan decided to visit the buffet table, needing a reason to excuse himself from the conversation with his wife and the Arnolds. He'd been there less than five minutes when he was approached.

"Ivan DeZhabi?"

Ivan set aside the small saucer of food he had prepared. "Yes?" he confirmed, smiling at the beautiful woman who stood at his side.

"I'm sorry. You don't know me. I'm Hester Morgan. I'm another one of GeFran's faces."

"Oh," Ivan said with a smile and extended his hand. "Very nice to meet you."

"Same here," Hester told him, her black eyes greedily studying every angle and curve of his devastatingly handsome honey-toned face. "Your wife is quite the beauty."

"Yes, she is." Ivan replied without hesitation, his raven-black stare growing sharper.

"And very lucky to be working for GeFran Cosmetics," Hester added, smiling when she noticed a muscle tighten in Ivan's jaw.

"Lucky?" he repeated, turning to retrieve his plate from the glass buffet table. "How so?"

Hester was all too happy to enlighten him. "Well, Frank and Geneva believe in keeping their girls busy. Especially the new ones. GeFran boasts offering the greatest exposure for up-and-coming models."

"So I've been told." Ivan sighed, as he munched on a stalk of celery and prayed for his agitation to abate.

"Mmm . . ." Hester held eye contact with Ivan as she reached around him to select a strawberry from a three-tiered porcelain platter. "They'll keep her jumping. She'll probably never have time to spare. That is, if they work her like they did me," she reminisced, while chewing on the plump sweet fruit. "I even had to break things off with my boyfriend at the time. I had nothing left to offer the guy once I was done with GeFran for the day."

"Not the kind of life for someone who already has a life, right?" Ivan guessed.

Hester's laughter rose softly in her throat. She let her

hand rest lightly against Ivan's chest and almost moaned at the feel of the unyielding wall of muscle beneath her palm. "Well, what I had was just a childish fling," she whispered. "Lawrencia is married and that's far more important than havin' some pictures in a magazine."

"Hmm . . ."

"Besides, I hear you're in advertising too. It's gotta keep you hopping."

"Definitely."

"You're with one of the agencies, right?" Hester inquired, though she already knew the answer.

Ivan slid one hand into his trouser pocket and smiled. "Cabron and McKenzie."

"Right," she said while she polished off the last of the strawberry. "That's interesting."

"What?"

"You just strike me as the type of man who would be running his own company, that's all," she commended subtly, caressing the swell of her bosom visible above the heart-shaped bodice of her burgundy gown.

"Thank you," Ivan replied. His dark eyes did not follow the seductive trail of Hester's fingers.

"Cabron and McKenzie, huh?" Hester taunted, hoping to spark something more between herself and Ivan before they were interrupted. "Tell you what, Mr. DeZhabi, you keep me in mind when you start calling models, all right?"

Ivan graced her with his incredible smile, before bowing his head. "You'll be first on my list."

Hester's gaze was desire personified as it lingered on his face. "Sounds good," she whispered, before sauntering away.

Ivan allowed his calm mask to fade and his frustration to appear.

* * *

The ride home from the Arnolds' estate was most unnerving. Rencia had sensed the change in Ivan's mood since their talk with Frank and Geneva. She'd expected him to express his feelings on the way back to Brooklyn, but he simply selected the Bilal CD and let the neo-soul grooves liven the trip home.

By the time the SUV was parked, Rencia had lost her desire to talk at all. Ivan waited for her to collect her things, then escorted her to their stoop. The ascent to the front door ended without conversation and Rencia headed straight for the stairs once they were inside.

"Larry."

Rencia bowed her head and closed her eyes. "Uh-huh?" she answered.

"I don't want you to do this," he said softly, watching as she turned to face him. "I don't want you to take this job."

"Why not?" Rencia demanded.

Ivan pulled the gray silk tie loose and jerked it from his collar, while unbuttoning his suit coat. "I just don't like it. I don't like thinking about what your working for GeFran would do to us."

"Do to us, Zhabi?" Rencia whispered, watching him as he headed toward the living room. "Or do to you?"

Ivan's steps drew to a halt. "Excuse me?"

"Frank and Geneva shot about a million holes in your argument against my working for them. You said modeling would be too unstable, but they've shown it would be just the opposite."

"Larry—"

"No, Ivan. You know, I told Geneva that I thought you were only against this type of work. That's not true, is it?"

Ivan's expression was as cold as ice. Still, he managed to keep his tone low as he spoke. "What are you trying to say?"

Rencia folded her arms across the snug bodice of her cream gown. "I'm saying that you simply don't want me to earn a living in any capacity."

"Damn it Larry, where is all this crap comin' from?" he suddenly exploded, raking a hand through his glossy jet-black locks. "Earn a living? A month ago, that was the last thing on your mind."

"And that's where you're wrong, Zhabi," Rencia corrected, her green gaze reflecting both regret and frustration. "This is something I've wanted for a long time. But this—this damned attitude of yours—is why I kept my feelings to myself."

Ivan practically ripped the buttons from his shirt collar as he pulled them loose. "Do you know how many women would kill to sit home all day and do nothing?" he argued, still unfastening his gray shirt.

Rencia winced at the unintentionally hurtful remark. "A lot fewer than you think, Zhabi. And the fact that you think I stay home doing nothing makes me want this even more."

Ivan's long lashes fluttered closed and he massaged his eyes. "Baby, I didn't mean to make it sound that way and I don't want to argue with you about this anymore."

"Then you'll support me?" she whispered, laying her hands flat against his chest.

Ivan's expression was guarded. "Saying I don't want to argue with you about this means I don't expect it to be an issue between us. Which means I expect you to drop it, forget it, Rencia."

"Just like that?"

"Just like that!" he bellowed, storming to the built-in bar in the corner of the den.

"Why is this such a problem for you?" she cried, following her husband around behind the bar.

Ivan turned slowly. He walked toward Rencia like a big cat stalking its prey. She unconsciously retreated, until the small of her back touched the oak bar counter. Ivan trapped her there, placing a hand on either side of her. Rencia tossed her head back and fixed him with a determined glare.

Slowly, Ivan brought his face closer to hers. His hand began a slow ascent from her waist up over the bodice of her gown.

Rencia swallowed past the lump that had suddenly developed in her throat. Her eyes focused on his mouth and suddenly nothing else mattered except his touch.

Ivan's lips tested the silken curve of her cheek, his nose following the same path. After an eternity, it seemed, he pressed a lingering kiss to her parted lips.

"I don't think you have any idea how much you mean to me," he said, showering her mouth with whisper-soft kisses.

"Zhabi, I—"

"Shh . . ." he urged, his tongue slipping past her lips to briefly stroke the even ridge of her teeth. "I don't want to argue with you. I hate when we fight. You should never have to hear me raise my voice to you," he whispered, his thumb brushing her nipple outlined against the material of her dress, as though it were crying out for more than just a simple touch.

Rencia's hands shook where they rested against the edges of the bar. She stood on the tips of her clear, strappy four-inch heels and trailed her mouth along his jaw. "Zhabi, please kiss me again," she moaned, more interested in his actions than his words.

Ivan barely brushed his mouth against hers. "You won't come to me with this again?"

"No," she moaned again, deciding to stop trying to change his outlook. "Please."

Ivan's smile epitomized satisfaction. He caught Rencia around her waist and pulled her up high against him. He kissed her passionately, his tongue thrusting deep and hard. Rencia wound her arms around his neck and slipped her fingers through his hair.

The rest of the night passed quickly, yet enjoyably.

After the night of the GeFran party, she made a decision to keep her business and personal life separate from her husband's. Though she hated not being able to share her success with him, she thought it best to let Ivan believe she had finally submitted to his way of thinking. The fact that their blossoming careers kept them so busy that they were like two ships passing in the night made it somewhat easier to continue the charade.

"How's the party comin'?" Ivan asked one evening after they'd finished the dinner dishes. He had suggested they make a point of getting together for at least one meal, and the evening had passed quite nicely.

Rencia, who hadn't thought once about the party in the last two weeks, came up with a quick response. "Kendra's and my schedules are so crazy we haven't been able to get together," she told him, knowing that it was only her schedule that was causing the delay.

Ivan leaned back in his chair and regarded his wife with a narrowed stare. "How could your schedule be in the way when you're home all day?"

Rencia pursed her lips and kept a tight rein on her heating temper. Ivan's comment made her want to lunge across the table at him. "There's a lot to be done around here, Zhabi, and besides, Kendra works."

"Yeah, I know," he replied tiredly.

Rencia frowned. "What?"

Ivan left the table and went to lean against the kitchen island. "You know, we're making our move soon and we wanted to snag a few contacts before we bounced," he explained.

Rencia nodded and scratched her temple lightly. "I see."

Ivan finished clearing the table. "Maybe we can set something up at a restaurant or something," he suggested.

Rencia gave him a sour look over the idea. "No, don't do that. Listen, I'm not promising anything fabulous, but I think I could get something set up for you in another couple of weeks if that'll work."

Ivan's head snapped up. "Not a problem. You think you can pull it off?"

"I think so, but I'll need your help, Zhabi," she warned.

Ivan raised his hands. "Anything," he promised.

"Okay then, you'll have to make out the guest list and contact everyone you want to attend."

Ivan shook his head. "No problem."

"Mmm-hmm," she countered. "I hope not, Zhabi." She sighed, hoisting herself atop the black marble countertop. "So the issue now is food and music. I suggest we cater, but just simple dishes, nothing outrageous."

"I agree," Ivan replied absently, his eyes focused on his wife's long legs dangling over the side of the counter.

"Any preferences?" she asked, as she leaned over to fill

a water glass from the faucet. "Zhabi?" she called when he offered no response.

"Oh, um, any food you choose is fine," he said, his hands caressing her bare thighs.

Rencia cleared her throat when she felt his fingers slipping beneath the edges of her snug shorts. "And the music?" she barely managed to ask.

Ivan squeezed her bottom, smiling when he discovered she wore no underwear. "Pick whatever you like."

"Sounds good. Maybe something Christmasy." She sighed, wanting nothing more than to stay and indulge in a few hours of sensual playtime with her husband. Unfortunately, she had an evening photo shoot and could not be late.

"I'll get back to you on this tomorrow," she told him, easing off the counter. Placing a quick peck on his cheek, she strolled out of the kitchen.

A warm, sexy smile softened Ivan's devastating features as he watched her leave. She seemed so different lately. He didn't know what it was, but he liked it a lot.

"Good morning, dear," Geneva Arnold greeted, meeting Rencia in the middle of her office.

"Geneva, Frank. Hey, Kent."

"Sweetheart, help yourself to some juice, muffins. We may be here awhile," Frank suggested.

"Pammy, the floor is yours."

Pammy Michaels, GeFran's marketing VP, rubbed her hands together. "Lawrencia, Geneva and Frank have probably told you most of what's going to be expected of you with regards to the Breeze campaign. You've already had several preliminary shoots. This portfolio outlines your more high-profile photo shoots for the next two and a half months."

"That long, huh?" Rencia lightly teased, scanning the lengthy list of dates and locales. "They're all in New York?" she asked, surprise and subtle relief tinging her words.

Pammy's round face carried a knowing look. "That's right. For the first couple of months, everything will be handled from the city. Holiday shoots, mostly. We don't have much time, but we'd like to salvage as much buzz during Christmas as possible. Afterward, once we get started with the commercial shoots and public appearances, your travel will be more widespread. We already have one scheduled for Cancún."

"I see."

"Any questions so far?" Geneva asked.

Rencia debated only a moment. "I know GeFran has an in-house agency. Will I be working exclusively with your people?"

"Funny you should ask that, Lawrencia," Kent Daniels replied. "We have been thinking of going with an outside ad agency on this."

"An outside agency?" Rencia repeated, recalling Ivan's conversation with Silas at her introduction party. "Any prospects yet?" She feared Cabron and McKenzie was a front runner for the job.

Kent glanced toward Pammy, who sat perched on the majestic pine desk. "We have been tossing around the idea of going with an outside firm, but there's nothing set in stone yet. We may even decide to ditch the idea completely."

Rencia nodded and silently prayed for them to do just that.

"Any more questions, dear?" Geneva asked, watching Rencia smile and shake her head.

Pammy scooted off the desk. "All right then, let's discuss your next shoot."

Chapter Five

One week later

Sam was in the midst of proofing a proposal when his private line buzzed. "This is Sam," he greeted quickly.

"Mr. Long? This is Pammy Michaels from GeFran Cosmetics."

Sam sat up in his brown leather desk chair. "Yes, Ms. Michaels, how are you?"

"Just fine, thanks for asking. Listen, I wanted to call about your proposal."

"You all have come to a decision already?"

"Mmm . . . not quite. The powers-that-be still have to decide whether they want the added expense of using an outside agency. This is, however, a very important campaign and because it took us so long to find the Breeze girl, I have a feeling they will definitely go for it."

Sam cleared his throat. "And what does that mean for me and my partner?"

"That means, should everything materialize as planned, DeZhabi-Long will be handling all TV spots for the Breeze fragrance."

* * *

"Ren, things may be goin' smooth as silk now, but don't get comfortable," Casey warned Rencia when they met to talk in her office.

"I know, Case, but I just don't feel like hearing it from Ivan right now," she groaned, tossing a paper plate into the wastebasket.

Casey blotted her lips with a napkin. "All right, all right. I just don't want all this to blow up in your face."

Rencia gave her friend a smile. "I know and it's not that I'm afraid to tell Ivan. I just want to go to him with my first cover in my hand when I tell him. It's funny, but now that I have something to do with myself, I feel so much stronger."

"I know what you mean," Casey interjected.

"Ivan just makes me so mad with this 'my word is final' mess. But I do realize that I have to tell him something and quick."

Casey frowned. "What's that all about?"

"My magazine spreads will begin to appear in another couple of weeks. It's more than I can count and Ivan's bound to see at least one of them," Rencia explained.

"Damn."

"Exactly," Rencia confirmed, just as her cell phone began to ring. "This is Lawrencia."

"Hello, dear, it's Geneva. Listen, I know it's short notice, but could you get away for lunch this afternoon?"

"Sure." Rencia replied quickly. "Did you want to meet somewhere?"

"The Tavern. Noon sharp."

"All right, I'll see you then," Rencia sang, before setting the shiny black receiver in its cradle. "Oh no," she whispered, the moment her fingers left the handset. She remembered she had a lunch date with Ivan and had no desire to call and cancel on him. Lately, things had been surprisingly wonderful. Of course, she acknowledged that the peace had much to do with her decision to keep her work a secret.

"Oh well, might as well get this over with," she groaned and pressed the button to speed-dial her husband's private line.

"Yeah?"

"Zhabi? Hey, it's me."

"I know," he whispered, his quiet voice growing even softer when he heard Rencia on the line. "What's up?"

"Um . . . I—I hate to do this, but . . . I need to cancel lunch," she blurted.

Ivan leaned back in his oversized black desk chair. "Something wrong?"

"Oh no, nothing like that, but there is something I need to take care of and I'd like to get it out of the way as soon as possible."

Ivan smiled and drew a line through the date he'd marked on his calendar. "Larry, it's okay. We can always do it another time."

Rencia cleared her throat. "We can?"

"Sure we can."

"Thank you, Zhabi." She sighed.

"We'll talk when I get home, all right?"

"Mmm-hmm."

Ivan shook his head once the connection broke. He could tell how uneasy she was over having to cancel out and he despised himself for being so difficult when they were dealing with the issue of her having a career.

"Hey, man, you got a minute?"

Ivan looked up and saw Sam peeking into the office. "What's up?" he called.

Sam closed the door, then strolled into the room with his arms folded across his wide chest. "I'm about to make your weekend. Guess who I just talked to?"

"How many guesses do I get?"

"None. I'll tell you: Pammy Michaels."

Ivan stroked his jaw and pretended to focus on the name.

"GeFran's marketing VP," Sam revealed.

Ivan's sleek brows rose a notch. "What's the verdict?"

"DeZhabi-Long has its first account. We'll be handling all TV spots for GeFran's new fragrance."

"Mmm." Ivan gestured, clenching his fist and pounding it on his desk in a display of sheer glee.

Sam was rubbing his hands together. "We're on our way, brotha. Looks like it paid off to take that tip about GeFran looking to an outside firm to promote this thing. Our first meeting will be in a couple of weeks and we'll meet the model and everyone."

"It's a good thing we decided to announce our resignations early," Ivan noted. "And with the party coming up, it would've been very awkward."

Sam shook his head. "I'll say. I have to admit, I was sure we'd be a couple of out-of-work advertisers for a while. But the firm's been good to us."

"Yeah, they've brought us a long way," Ivan agreed.

"Mmm," Sam said, "a very long way. DeZhabi-Long is an upstart firm with no credentials. GeFran taking a chance on us was a true blessing."

"Hmph."

"Hmph? What's that about?"

Ivan looked down at his tie and studied the gold flecks sprinkled across the beige silk. "It's just ironic, that's all."

"What is?"

"Rencia was suppose to be working for GeFran. Instead, I am."

Sam smoothed one hand across his bald head. "She did what you wanted, kid."

"I know, but still . . ."

"You feelin' guilty?"

"No, hell no," Ivan denied in an uneasy tone and bolted from his chair.

Sam toyed with the tiny race cars littering a corner of Ivan's desk. "What is it, then?"

Ivan couldn't admit that he was feeling extremely guilt-ridden over coercing his wife into turning down something she seemed to want so much.

"I'm gonna take her away for the weekend," he decided, sounding as though he were speaking to himself.

"Mmm, yeah, doin' somethin' like that will definitely help with the guilt."

Ivan fixed his partner with a murderous glare.

"DeZhabi? DeZhabi-Long? I—I had no idea that they were even in the running for the account."

Geneva shrugged and sprinkled fresh-ground black pepper on her crisp chef salad. "Well, they approached us with a proposal shortly after announcing their resignations from Cabron and McKenzie. They impressed us far more than any of the other candidates. I think that was because they were the most hungry for it. An upstart firm, two headstrong young men out to make a name for themselves. I'm impressed by their ambition and shrewdness—taking on the account for themselves instead of sharing the wealth with Cabron and McKenzie. Yes, they are two very impressive young men."

"Is that right?" Rencia inquired dryly.

"I don't expect you to believe this, but we didn't pick Ivan's agency because of you. We wanted to go with a small firm, and Ivan and his partner gave a phenomenal presentation."

Rencia raked all ten of her fingers through her stunning mane. "I know, I know. My husband is very good at what he does."

"But you don't know if you can work with him?"

"Hmph," Rencia grunted, unable to tell Geneva just how outrageous the idea seemed in light of the fact that Ivan didn't even know she was working at all. "Everyone isn't as comfortable in that area as you and Frank."

"Oh, sweetie, I know," Geneva cooed, reaching across the table to pat Rencia's hand. "Think about it this way, you'll get to enjoy both business and pleasure with that sexy, gorgeous husband of yours."

Geneva's naughty remarks did little to soothe Rencia's nerves. Ivan was under the impression that she had given up the idea of working. Telling him that she had taken the job and, moreover, would be working closely with him filled her with a sense of dread.

Chapter Six

The Marsh Inn's Connecticut location made for a perfect getaway, especially during the autumn and winter seasons. Ivan and Rencia usually visited the establishment on their anniversary, so nothing had prepared Rencia for the impromptu trip.

"Zhabi . . . what in the world are we doing here?" Rencia gasped, amazement luminating her face as she gazed upon the cozy, rustic bed-and-breakfast inn.

Ivan's grin revealed his dimples, but he pretended to sound hurt. "Damn, do I need a reason to bring you up here?"

"No . . ." Rencia quickly denied, turning her eyes toward her husband. "No, Zhabi, we just haven't visited this place in a while, that's all."

"Over a year," he clarified, leaning across the console and cupping her neck with a massive hand. "I think we're due for a visit, don't you?"

Rencia felt as though she were drowning in the bottomless depths of Ivan's onyx stare. She barely managed a nod, her lips parting when he moved closer.

Ivan brushed his thumb across her cheek as his mouth settled in for a kiss. He stroked the lush curve of her lips with the tip of his tongue, then thrust deep inside.

"Zhabi," she breathed, allowing him to add more pressure to the kiss. A tiny whimper rose in her throat and she eagerly returned the gesture.

"We should go in," Ivan decided when he broke the kiss. His incredibly handsome features softened again when he glimpsed the disappointment on his wife's face. "Don't worry, I intend to finish what I started."

Rencia's lashes fluttered as she rolled her eyes and landed a playful push to one of Ivan's unyielding shoulders.

"We're going to have dinner?" she asked, when they stepped inside the suite. She eyed the intimate round table set for two.

Ivan locked the door behind the bellman. "Later," he informed her, removing his stylishly rugged snow-white bomber jacket.

Rencia pulled the fuzzy fuschia knit cap from her head and set about removing the matching gloves and black cashmere overcoat as she inspected the room.

"Have a drink with me?" Ivan asked, watching her as she gazed into the roaring flame in the living room fireplace. Ivan filled two champagne flutes to the rim with the bubbly amber liquid. When he handed Rencia her glass, she giggled.

"Champagne? Zhabi, what's going on?"

"What?" he cried, feigning confusion. He bowed his head, allowing the heavy midnight twists to shield one side of his handsome face.

Rencia went to stand directly before him and smiled up at him. "You know, you can't fool me. Spill it," she ordered.

Ivan's easy expression grew a tad leery. "I'm not sure how you're gonna take what I have to tell you."

Blinking, Rencia tilted her head and regarded him with curious eyes. "I guess you won't know that until you tell me."

Ivan took a sip of his champagne and nodded. "I told you I'd given my resignation to the firm. What I didn't tell you was that Sam and I were also working on obtaining our first account. We got that account today."

Rencia felt her hand tighten around the delicate crystal stem. "Congratulations," she managed.

Ivan drained his glass and set it aside. "I hope you feel that way once you hear who it is," he said, watching her shrug. "GeFran Cosmetics."

Rencia swallowed past the lump lodged in her throat. "GeFran?"

"Yeah."

"Congratulations, Zhabi. I meant it when I said it before."

Ivan folded his arms across the denim shirt hanging outside his cream corduroy trousers. "It doesn't bother you knowing I'm working for a company I suggested you not work for?"

"You didn't suggest, Zhabi. You outright told me you weren't havin' it."

"Larry—"

"Zhabi, what is it that you expect me to say? 'Don't do it'? 'I forbid it'? Unlike you, I don't have an issue with you having a life outside our marriage."

Ivan bowed his head and massaged the bridge of his nose. "I didn't bring you all the way up here to argue."

"Then can we please drop it?" she urged, turning away to observe the flames searing the heavy logs in the fireplace.

Ivan pushed both hands into his deep pockets and followed her across the room. He stood right behind Rencia and dipped his head to press a soft kiss to the shell of her ear. His lips slid down to suckle the soft lobe, his tongue soothing the area where his perfect teeth had nipped.

Rencia was torn between anger and arousal. She wanted time to remain aloof and silent, but Ivan was making that impossible. Her long lashes fluttered like a hummingbird's wings as her body succumbed to his incredible touch.

Ivan could feel her softening and mercilessly continued the sensual attack on her hormones. He continued to suck and nibble on her earlobe while extracting his hands from his pockets to settle them against her hips.

Rencia curved one hand over the back of the cocoa-colored armchair situated close to the fire. The other curved into a fist and her nails threatened to break the skin of her palm while she struggled to restrain her emotions.

"Zhabi, please," she whispered, when he unfastened her jeans. "We shouldn't do this now."

Ivan did not stop. "Has there ever been a time we haven't come here and not made love?" he queried, grinning at the gasp she uttered when his hand disappeared inside her panties.

"We should talk, I have to tell you—"

"Shh . . ."

Rencia's gasp transformed itself into a helpless whimper and she winced in pleasure when her husband's fingers entered her body. She drew her lower lip between her teeth and fought to smother the wanton moan building in her throat.

"You can't possibly want me to stop," he taunted, as he rotated his fingers in the rich creaminess bathing his skin. His other hand found her breast, fondling and squeezing one before turning his attention to its twin.

After a while, Rencia could no longer hide her response to Ivan's touch. She gasped his name torturedly as orgasmic waves of pleasure welled inside her. Ivan only increased the speed of his thrusting and rotating fingers. Rencia's head fell back against his shoulder and she allowed the sensations to overwhelm her. Ivan continued to stroke her intimately even as she moaned that she couldn't stand anymore.

"Zhabi, wait," she cautioned, when he turned her to face him.

"Shh . . ." he commanded again, pulling the charcoal-gray sweater over her head before going to his knees to remove her jeans, boots, and undergarments.

When Rencia stood completely nude before him, Ivan worshipped her beauty with his eyes, then his hands, and finally his mouth. He cupped her full bottom and feasted upon the center of her body. Rencia feared her nails would pierce the taut skin of his massive shoulders, she held on to him so tightly. She experienced another incredible orgasm, which left her as limp as a rag doll.

Ivan, however, wasn't done yet. He carried her to the bedroom and placed her in the center of the canopied king-size bed. Rencia wanted to give in to the drowsiness weighing on her eyelids, but that was not to be. Ivan casually removed his clothes, then slipped between the crisp white bed linens.

"Zhabi, I can't," she moaned, when his considerable weight covered her. She couldn't recall the last time she'd felt so ravished. "Baby, just a tiny nap," she pleaded, gasping when his lips closed over the tip of one breast.

Ivan smiled at her reaction. "You'll get one," he promised.

Rencia cried out unashamed as he entered her. Her long legs curled around Ivan's wide muscular back as she stretched her arms above her head and savored the devastating power and stamina of his body.

The weekend passed in a blissful blur. Several times, Rencia was at the brink of informing her husband that they were both working for the same company. Unfortunately, experiencing such enjoyment with Ivan after so many weeks of constant work made her reluctant to spoil any aspect of their time together. She ignored the small voice warning that waiting longer could make things worse.

While Ivan got dressed for work, exactly one week after their lovely stay at the bed-and-breakfast, he kept watching his wife. She was sitting Indian-style in the middle of their huge bed with a pad in her hand. The party for the company would be that evening, and Rencia was going over a few last-minute details. As Ivan studied her frowning over a pad, a slow smile tugged at his mouth.

It had been impossible to ignore the subtle yet noticeable change in her demeanor. She had always captivated him, whatever the situation. Now it was as if he were . . . entranced. There was a confidence surrounding her lately that he had never seen before.

Meanwhile, Rencia was giving herself a mental pat on the back for putting together the party in such a hurry and she was focused on putting the party behind her. Then she could concentrate on more important things, like telling her husband that she was now a member of the workforce and he would have to deal with it. The mood from the trip had carried over once they'd returned home, and while she hated to ruin that, the time for coddling her husband had ended.

"Ivan?" she called in a firm voice.

"Yeah," he replied from the dresser where he stood setting his watch.

"You did contact all your guests, didn't you?" she asked, holding her breath.

Ivan gave a short laugh and shook his head. "Yeah, Larry, it's all taken care of."

"I don't know why I bothered to ask you now. It's the beginning of December." She sighed. "Well, that's that." She placed a huge check mark over the pad.

Ivan cleared his throat then and stepped closer to the bed. "So do you think it'll turn out all right?" he asked, watching her closely.

Rencia pushed a lock of hair behind her ear. "Oh, I think it'll turn out better than all right. This party is gonna be so good, you two may wind up stealing all of Cabron and McKenzi's clients," she predicted.

Ivan's long dark brows rose in an impressed gesture. "I'm surprised they didn't call for it to be canceled once Sam and I handed in our resignations."

"They're a good firm, I think their clients know they're in good hands," Rencia noted. "Still, DeZhabi-Long is going to provide them with some stiff competition."

Ivan grinned. "You think so?"

"I know so."

"Where's all this comin' from, Larry?" he asked, crossing his arms over his chest.

Rencia shrugged, still looking at her pad. "All of what?"

Ivan pulled the pad from her fingers and tossed it to the other side of the bed. Placing his hands on either side of her, he forced her to lie down. "This confidence," he clarified.

Rencia's eyes widened slightly, but she shook her head. "Is there something wrong with being confident?"

Ivan lowered his head. "No, but all of a sudden you've come into a truckload of it."

"Don't you like it?" she asked, the tone of her voice as intense and seductive as the look in her stare.

Ivan's gaze took a heated trip over the luscious length of Rencia's scantily clad body. When his eyes reached her face again, he nodded. "Oh yes," he assured her, as his head lowered to hers.

A soft whimper escaped Rencia's lips as Ivan's mouth settled on hers. He eased his tongue slowly and deeply inside, smiling when he heard her moan. He touched her nowhere else, but she couldn't complain. The mastery of his mouth was potent and each leisurely stroke forced another cry past her lips.

"Ivan?" she finally called. "Zhabi?"

"What?" he asked, between kisses.

Rencia's hands caressed the softness of his hair and she sighed. "You know you'll be late for work if we keep this up, right?"

Ivan was silent for a moment, before he finally raised his head. "Damn you."

Rencia laughed as she watched him reluctantly move away. Before he moved too far, she grabbed his arm.

"Zhabi?" she called, deciding to bite the bullet and finally tell him about her own job.

Ivan turned toward her and smiled. "What, baby?"

Rencia stared up at him for a long moment. Then her courage failed her again. "I'll see you tonight."

Ivan tugged on a lock of her hair before he kissed her forehead. Then he was gone.

Rencia pounded her fist against the cushioned comforter of the bed.

Tate Green pulled off her gray pumps and groaned. As she massaged her aching toes, she watched the two gorgeous men who inspected the office.

"Tate? You okay over there?" Sam called to the real estate broker he and Ivan had hired.

Tate nodded. "Yeah, if this is a girl, she's not gonna like heels very much," she said, patting her swollen belly.

"You could deliver that baby any day. Why are you still working, anyway?" Ivan asked in a low, moody voice as he studied the standard burgundy carpeting.

Tate rolled her eyes toward him. "Why are you two wasting my time with the place?"

Ivan pretended to be offended. "You don't like it?"

"Do you?" Tate challenged.

Ivan pushed his large hands into the deep pockets of his stylish cocoa trousers. "I love it! Don't you, Sam?"

Sam turned to Tate and spread his hands. "Hell yeah, what's your problem, girl?"

Tate ran a hand over her dark brown hair. "Well, this was my third choice," she said.

"Well, it should've been your first," Sam muttered.

Tate's dark face was a picture of confusion. "I can't believe you guys didn't like either of my earlier suggestions," she said, looking around the quaint Brooklyn office. "I know you guys can afford . . . better."

"Well, you sold us on this one. So you can tell us where to sign or we can get somebody else to take the commission," Ivan teased.

Tate, who had known Ivan and Sam since before she left Cabron and MacKenzie to pursue a career in real estate, placed a tight smile on her face and raised her hands. "Cheapskates," she accused, laughing when they both stared at her with hurt expressions. Turning too quickly, she knocked her open briefcase from the counter where it rested. "Damn," she mumbled.

Sam and Ivan moved Tate away from the briefcase before she could stoop to retrieve it. As they gathered the papers strewn across the carpet, Ivan's attention was drawn to the magazine lying open in the briefcase. His first thought was that the girl on the page was unquestionably beautiful. So much so that he wanted to take a closer look. Intrigued, he picked up the magazine and focused on the page. His mouth fell open when he saw that it was Rencia's face gracing the glossy page. He glanced at the cover before replacing the magazine in the briefcase.

"I think we made a good choice, man," Sam said as he and Ivan drove back to the firm.

Ivan had his chin resting on his fist and kept his face averted to the window.

"So next week, we'll be on our way out of Cabron and MacKenzie," Sam continued.

"Mmm-hmm . . . " Ivan agreed absently.

Sam frowned and finally glanced over at his friend. "Man, what is your problem?"

Ivan was about to answer when he spied a newsstand on an approaching corner. "Hey, stop the car!" he ordered.

Sam parked his SUV a few feet from the curb and got

out to follow Ivan to the magazine stand. "Man, what the devil is wrong with you?"

Ivan purchased a magazine and was staring unblinkingly at his wife's photo.

Sam peered over Ivan's shoulder and laughed. "Damn, I didn't know Rencia took the modeling gig. Why'd you keep it a secret?"

Ivan slammed the magazine shut. "Damn it," he muttered, walking away.

Rencia opened her front door to Casey, who sprinted inside the house waving a magazine.

"Hot damn, Ren! Girl, this spread is gorgeous!" she bellowed. Rencia frowned and watched Casey as though the woman had gone mad. "What are you talkin' about?"

Casey fixed her friend with an uneasy stare. "Don't tell me you haven't seen this?" she questioned, holding out the latest edition of *Nubia* magazine.

Rencia snatched it from Casey and thumbed through the pages. Shock and happiness brightened her face when she saw the layout. "Oh Lord, I had no idea this would be out today!"

"Dang, I wish I could see the look on Ivy's face when you tell him!" Casey said.

Happy could only begin to describe the way Rencia felt. In spite of his feelings toward her working, she was sure her husband would be just as elated as she was when she told him about the magazine. She couldn't wait until that night.

Around six that evening, Rencia was laying her dress across the bed. The firm's party would be starting in less that two hours and it promised to be fantastic. She'd been running around all day making last-minute changes and putting the finishing touches on the house. Luckily, it hadn't taken long to get most of the work out of the way. With all that was going on, it was difficult to keep herself focused.

When Casey walked into the house waving the magazine, she couldn't have been more surprised. Everything seemed to be happening so quickly. One day she was wondering what she'd do with the rest of her life, and the next day she was a highly paid model. Rencia sighed as she took a seat at her vanity dresser. Deciding to wear her hair in a French roll, she set about the task of brushing her locks away from her face.

The front door slammed a few seconds later, but she didn't veer from her task. She knew it must have been Ivan and a smile brightened her face. She couldn't wait to tell him her news.

Unfortunately, Rencia had no clue about her husband's mood. Instead of heading right upstairs, he detoured to the den. Fixing himself a stiff drink behind the bar, he willed his temper to cool. Of course, the two cognacs he tossed back did little to soothe his anger. He couldn't believe Rencia had actually gone behind his back and taken that job, especially when she already knew how he felt about it. Ivan never once thought he was being unfair to his wife. It never occurred to him that his behavior might begin to push her away. The only thing he cared about was that she had lied to him.

Rencia eyed herself in the mirror. Satisfied with the results, she nodded. She had wrapped most of her hair into the classy roll, while other silky tendrils lay along the side of her face and neck. She had just slipped into her dress when she heard Ivan bounding up the stairs. The sleek gold silk gown clung to her every heart-stopping curve in a most adoring manner. The dress had thin straps and a bra-styled bodice and the deep front split offered unforgettable glimpses of her shapely legs and thighs.

The bedroom door flew open, but Rencia didn't bother to turn around. Instead, she waved toward her back. "Zhabi, baby, could you zip this for me?" she requested.

Ivan ran a large hand across his locks secured into a ponytail, then, with a light tug on Rencia's upper arms, he turned her around to face him. His eyes roamed her body coldly, and then he motioned for her to sit on the bed.

"What is wrong with you?" Rencia cried, a dark frown clouding her face.

Ivan pointed at her. "You lied to me."

Rencia was speechless; her eyes were wide as she gazed up at him. Ivan made a disgusted sound in his throat and grabbed his chocolate overcoat. He pulled a copy of *Nubia* magazine from the deep inside pocket and tossed it next to his wife on the bed.

Rencia expelled the breath she'd been holding and shook her head. "I was gonna tell you tonight," she declared.

Ivan gave a short laugh. "Yeah, I'll bet."

Rencia massaged her temples. "I didn't mean for you to find out this way," she told him, staring at the magazine.

Ivan sat down next to her and leaned forward to brace his elbows on his knees. "You didn't mean for me to find out *this* way? What were you gonna say, Larry? 'Oh, Zhabi, by the way, I went behind your back and took that job'? Is that what you were gonna tell me?"

Rencia looked at him as though he were crazy. "Behind your back? Damn it, Zhabi, I told you everything there was to tell!"

"And I told you no!"

"Who the hell do you think you are, my father?" she countered, her eyes spewing arrows of fire.

If possible, Ivan's gaze turned even more intense. He moved away from the bed and began jerking out of his clothes. "You let me think you were gonna forget about this crap," he grumbled.

Rencia smoothed her hands across her thighs. "I let you think that because I was sick of beating my head against the wall trying to make you understand why I wanted to do this."

Ivan pulled the cream shirt away from his chiseled chest. "Larry, thanks for clearing that up for me now."

Rencia left the bed. "Damn it, Ivan, I didn't just outright lie the way you did," she cooly pointed out.

Ivan tossed the clothes in the corner and turned. "What is that supposed to mean?"

"Are you forgetting about how you first promised to support me when I told you about all this?"

Ivan glanced away, just as Rencia glimpsed the guilty expression in his eyes. "Larry, you've been working for GeFran since October. How could you keep that from me this long? Especially after I told you that we got the account."

"I was trying to find the right time to get into it," she said, grimacing at how weak the reply sounded. When Ivan snorted his disbelief, she snapped, "I wouldn't have had to keep this a secret if I had something besides a selfish, old-fashioned bastard for a husband!" she cried, feeling her heart thudding in anticipation when Ivan went still.

Rencia held her ground, even when Ivan's gaze narrowed. She eagerly awaited his rebuttal, but it was not forthcoming. After a moment, he simply turned and headed into the bathroom. The door slammed viciously behind him.

Chapter Seven

As Rencia hoped, the party turned out to be a success. Everyone Ivan had invited showed up ready to have a good time. Though it was still a bit early, the house was already beautifully lit and decorated for the approaching Christmas holiday. Last-minute jitters had Rencia wondering if their brownstone could handle so many guests, but she needn't have worried, everything worked out perfectly.

Everything, that is, except her and Ivan's moods. They hadn't spoken to one another since the argument earlier. As a result, none of the guests saw them together during the party. Casey was the only one who noticed the distance between them. Of course, she wasn't about to let the evening go by without questioning it.

Rencia was standing near the stereo arguing with Sam Long over his music selections. Casey caught up with her there.

"Lisa, will you please ask this man to play something besides all this rap?" Rencia pleaded, clasping her hands together.

"Girl, did you forget this is a party?" Sam asked, pretending to be aggravated.

Rencia rolled her eyes toward the ceiling. "I know it's a party, and since you're the designated DJ, you need to play what the guests wanna hear. I want to hear something else."

"Such as what, Ren?" he challenged, raising his hands above his head.

"Well . . . let's see, there's a big holiday approaching . . . I have it! Christmas music."

Sam chuckled.

"And I see you hiding that Kem over there. Put that on," she suggested.

Sam shook his head. "See? That goes to show how little you know about parties. You save your best stuff for last. But if you want to hear it now, fine."

Rencia folded her arms across her chest. "Thank you."

Meanwhile, Sam's girlfriend, Lisa Miller, was laughing uncontrollably. "Y'all are too much!" she cried.

"That's Sam."

"That's Rencia."

They spoke simultaneously.

"Excuse me, I hate to break this up," Casey said, laying her hand on Rencia's shoulder. "Can I talk to you a minute, girl?"

Rencia smiled at Casey before turning back to Sam. "I'll be back when this CD's through," she promised.

"I'll make sure not to be here," Sam retorted, enjoying their relentless teasing.

Casey pulled Rencia along with her to the downstairs bathroom, located just off from the den. "What's goin' on with you and Ivy?"

Rencia didn't pretend to misunderstand. "He saw the magazine before I had a chance to tell him about it," she said, then recalled the awful argument.

Casey replied with a heavy sigh. "Damn . . . so what now? You two just gonna ignore each other all evening?"

Rencia shrugged her slender shoulders. "I guess. . . ."

"Ren—"

"Listen, Case, I may have been wrong to keep what I was doing a secret, but Ivan was just as wrong for forbidding me to work and lying about supporting me in whatever I decided to do."

"True, but he hasn't spoken to you all night," Casey noted. "Do you really think he'll let it go at the slamming of a bathroom door?"

"No, but I'm not gonna waste my time worrying about it. If he wants to catch an attitude over this, then that's his problem."

The two friends talked awhile longer, before heading back into the party. Rencia had invited some people and was happy to see Kent Daniels and Silas Timmons walking into her home. She rushed over to meet them.

"I'm so glad you could make it!" she cried, hugging the two men.

Silas grinned. "Hey, working for GeFran makes you never want to turn down a party!" he called over the music.

Rencia pretended to be offended. "It's not so bad."

"Speak for yourself," Ken chimed in.

The laughing threesome never noticed Ivan watching them from across the room. He had been trying desperately to concentrate on entertaining his guests, but it was impossible. It had been his intention to keep his distance from Rencia that night. He'd literally closed the door on their conversation and decided to walk away before things got even more out of hand.

Ivan's attention returned to Rencia's new guests. He had recognized Kent and Silas and decided to walk over and greet them. Rencia was laughing over a comment when she felt a delicious caress tracing her spine. Look-

ing up into Ivan's intense gaze caused her heart to
pound.

"Zhabi," she whispered, surprised that he'd walked
over.

The deep dimple in the corner of Ivan's mouth appeared as he smiled. "You gonna hog Kent and Silas all
evening, babe?" he teased softly.

After a moment, Rencia smiled and shook her head.
"Oh no. Um, Kent, Silas, you got one half of your advertising team here," she gushed.

"What's up, man?" Kent and Silas both said as they
shook hands with Ivan, who returned the greeting.

"Kent and Silas were just telling me that our first meeting would be next week," Rencia explained as Ivan
turned toward her. She stood and waited for the in-
evitable explosion, but it never arrived.

Ivan, Kent, and Silas talked business as though they'd
been working together for years. Soon, Ivan was telling
them he'd introduce them to Sam before they left the
party. Then he patted Rencia's waist and walked away.
Her eyes lingered on her husband, admiring the fit of
the black trousers and matching jacket he wore over a
black crew shirt. Dismissing the path of her thoughts,
she looked away and tried to focus on something else.

"Curtis, we're glad you stayed so long. I didn't think
you'd be able to handle a party like this."

Curtis Henderson smiled at Ivan's teasing remark.
"Well, Kendra reminded me that we hadn't been out
dancing in a long time and I knew we'd get to do that
here. And since we're competitors now, we probably
won't have much time to socialize."

"Competitors, but still friends," Ivan corrected, reaching out to shake Curtis's hand.

Curtis laughed. "Damn right," he agreed. "Only a friend would throw a party like this for a new competitor. I think Rencia's decision to do something fun and laid-back helped Michaels to make up his mind. He's coming in to sign tomorrow morning," he commented, referring to the client he'd succeeded in wooing.

Ivan extended his hand. "Congratulations," he said, pleased that his employment with Cabron and McKenzie would end on a high note.

Curtis and his wife were the last guests to leave the party. When Rencia and Kendra made their way from the den to the front of the house, the Hendersons said their good-byes and left. The light mood that had been floating through the house left with them.

Rencia busied herself putting dishes into the washer, while Ivan straightened the den and living room.

Rencia remained in the kitchen much longer than necessary. She hoped that by the time she headed upstairs, Ivan would already be in bed and asleep. After every dish was safely tucked away in the oak cabinets, she turned out the lights and crept out of the kitchen.

"Larry," Ivan called from the den.

Rencia grasped the banister a little tighter and bowed her head. "What, Zhabi?" she whispered, a sense of déjà vu washing over her as she recalled an argument that had begun much the same way.

"Could you come in here?" he requested softly, leaning against the doorjamb.

Rencia took a deep breath and turned to do as he asked. When she was inside the den, he folded his arms. "How long are you gonna keep this up?" he asked.

Rencia's green stare was direct as she glared at him. "Keep what up?"

Ivan ran his hand across his face and sighed. "This modeling, Larry. How far do you plan to take this mess?"

Rencia winced at his words. "Oh, I don't know, probably until I'm about fifty. What do you think?" she inquired flippantly.

"Don't play with me, Larry," he groaned.

"Oh, Zhabi, the last thing I want to do is play with you. How can you just demand that I give this up?"

"Larry, I'm your husband and I told you—"

"You told me? Baby, I'm as old as you are. You don't have the right to *tell* me anything." She whispered, but her tone was firm.

Ivan's gaze reflected his surprise. "What is wrong with you?"

"Nothing. Not one thing is wrong with me. All I want to do is have a career. It's you who's turning this into a battle."

Ivan took offense. "I'm turning this into a battle?"

Rencia clenched her fists in response to the harsh tone of his voice.

Ivan closed the distance between them. Massaging the strong curve of his jaw, he bowed his head. "How am I turning this into a battle?" he whispered.

Rencia's brows drew closed and she watched him in disbelief. "I don't know how you can ask me that. Walkin' around here huffin' and puffin' about how I defied you, disobeyed you. Zhabi, you're acting like a monster about this. I mean, what type of working relationship do you hope for us to have if you can't get past your feelings about this?"

Ivan's long lashes closed over his intense stare and he turned away. When he said nothing more, Rencia expressed a frustrated sigh and stormed from the den. She headed upstairs and quickly stripped off her gown. After slipping into a short nightshirt, she headed to one of the guest bedrooms to sleep.

When Ivan finally arrived upstairs, Rencia had just fallen asleep. He went into their bedroom to undress, then he too headed out. He found her in the room across the hall. The locked door proved to be of no consequence for him. One powerful hand curled around the brass knob and he easily twisted it open. A weary look began to cloud his sensual features, but he couldn't let the night end on such a note. He moved closer to the bed. When he flipped the covers back, Rencia awakened.

"No, Ivan," she softly yet firmly ordered, pressing her hands against his wide chest. It was like pressing against a tree. "Ivan, get away from me," she called in a warning tone.

No hint of emotion crossed his face. "Come back to bed, Larry," he urged, taking her wrist.

"Go," she ordered.

"Don't make me beg," he said against her hair and lifted her from the covers to carry her out of the room.

He closed the bedroom door, before placing his wife in their bed and lying next to her. "I'm sorry," he whispered.

Rencia rolled her eyes, not wanting to be swayed by the sincere expression on his face.

"I'm sorry," he whispered again, a bit more intensely that time. He took both her hands in one palm and pressed them against his heart. When she gasped, he lowered his mouth to hers and thrust his tongue deep inside. She tried to nip at his tongue with her perfect teeth. Ivan felt the offending gesture and simply deepened the kiss.

"Please don't fight me, Larry, please."

Rencia felt tears of frustration pressuring her eyes. "We can't solve things this way."

Ivan broke the kiss and hid his handsome face in the side of her neck. "I know, and I'm not trying to, but I am sorry. I'm sorry for what I've been putting you through and I'll try to accept this, just please stop fighting me."

Rencia couldn't be sure if Ivan's words were brought on by the moment or something deeper, but she was tired of fighting too. Ivan's gentleness and his seductive power gradually won her over. Soon, he'd discarded her nightshirt and a soft cry passed her lips when she felt her body betray her mind. With a will of their own, her long, shapely legs shifted for him.

Ivan settled his lean, athletic form between her thighs and deepened the kiss. His hair brushed her skin as his head fell upon her chest. Warm persuasive lips and white teeth nibbled on the very tip of her breast. His face was shielded from her view by the glossy black locks of his hair.

After a while, neither could resist the overwhelming desire for satisfaction. Ivan heard Rencia softly plead with him to stop teasing her and he wasted no time. A groan rumbled within his chest when he sank into the creaminess of her body. His long thrusts began slow, and then grew faster. Rencia wouldn't have dreamed of pushing him away at that point. Ivan kept a firm hold on her wrists. Though completely unnecessary, the gesture only added more heat to the erotic act taking place between the tangled sheets.

Chapter Eight

"What the hell are y'all doin'?" Ivan shouted at the television. He was in the den watching highlights from the basketball game he'd missed the night before. Unfortunately, his team lost.

The doorbell rang, interrupting his harsh critique of the New York team. He cursed his way to the foyer, and there was a hellish frown darkening his face when he swung open the front door.

The young deliveryman wore an uneasy expression as he stared at the huge man with the black bandana tied over his head. "Delivery for Lawrencia De—DeZhabi?" he announced weakly.

Ivan sighed. "She's my wife. I'll sign for it," he offered, taking the pen from the young man's shaking hand and placing his name on the pad. The messenger handed him a large, flat cardboard package. Ivan set it next to the wall and when he turned back to the door, the man was hurrying away.

"Hey, wait a minute!" Ivan called.

"Yes, sir?"

Ivan reached into the pocket of his sagging jeans. He pulled out a ten-dollar bill and slapped it into the man's hand. "Thanks."

Ivan took the package along with him to the den. He

knew Rencia would come down on him for opening it, but since she was already angry with him, he didn't see the harm in it. Tearing through the heavy cardboard with strong fingers, he pulled out the glossy display of poster-sized photos. A sexy smirk tugged at his mouth as he studied his wife's work. He couldn't look away from the seductive vision she cast. He had to admit that the voluptuous beauty certainly had what it took to be a model. A supermodel, no less. Taking one of the mammoth-sized photos from the floor, Ivan decided to display it above the mantel in the den.

A few moments later, Rencia arrived downstairs. In spite of the closeness they'd shared the night before, she was determined to continue their conversation. When she saw Ivan in the den, staring at the poster, her words escaped her.

Ivan heard Rencia come into the room and glanced at her. A soft smile curved his mouth when he noticed the awed expression on her face. Turning, he leaned next to her and pressed his lips to her ear.

"Very nice," he said softly before leaving the room.

Rencia's mouth fell open at the unexpected compliment. Her eyes widened as a smile brightened her face.

Rencia's career had taken off like a rocket. Tons of magazine covers and layouts filled the house. Just over a month after the Breeze campaign was under way, there were already offers to appear in music videos.

Through it all, Ivan bit his tongue. Although he couldn't deny Rencia's natural flair, he didn't like her modeling at all. Still, he couldn't ignore the obvious: his wife had never appeared more radiant.

* * *

GeFran advertising and administrative executives, Sam, Ivan, and Rencia occupied the spacious top-floor conference room on New Year's Eve. Schedule conflicts had prevented the group from an earlier meeting. With everyone excited over the festive holiday, all eyes were focused on the fifty-four-inch screen for the viewing of the first TV spot for Breeze.

The concept of the commercial featured Rencia in a flower-filled meadow at the break of day. The sun rose and cast its golden glow upon hundreds of vibrant yellow tulips. The rays of light kissed Rencia's thick brown curls, which flew wildly against the breeze. The camera slowly panned around, briefly capturing the curve of her cheek, the line of her jaw and temple. The shot also caught her brilliant gaze just as she looked directly into the camera. Then white light filled the screen and a shot of the stout glass bottle carrying the Breeze logo and the product slogan appeared on the screen nestled amidst a sea of snow, before the shot faded to black.

"Beautiful," Frank complimented after a few moments of silence.

Geneva seemed to be in awe. "The camera captured just enough of her face to intrigue the viewer."

"We felt keeping the spot simple yet captivating would intrigue the consumer with not only Rencia's beauty, but also with the product," Sam explained.

The rest of the group obviously agreed, for a round of applause filled the room then. While everyone raved over the finished advertisement that would begin the very next week, Ivan and Rencia seemed preoccupied. He had barely glimpsed the commercial during its

thirty-second airing. His midnight eyes were more focused on his wife, who sat on the opposite side of the
long table, a few spaces down. Rencia could feel the
intensity of Ivan's stare as though he were actually
touching her. The desire radiating from his striking
coal-colored gaze reminded her of the look in his eyes
the evening they had spent at their special Connecticut bed-and-breakfast. More than anything, Rencia
wished she could recreate that special weekend.
Though they had worked closely on the Breeze campaign, they had little time left to be close on a more
personal level. As the face of Breeze, Rencia realized
that her job didn't end with fittings and photo sessions,
it only began there.

"Good work, Lawrencia."

"Thanks, Matt," she replied with a smile and waved toward the other ad execs who had just passed. She stood
to gather her things when she felt a hand press against
the small of her back.

"Congratulations," Ivan whispered, when she turned
to face him.

Rencia shrugged and smoothed one hand across her
snug burgundy pants. "Same to you. The commercial
came out wonderfully."

Ivan slipped one hand into the deep pocket of his
olive-green trousers. "That was because of you," he said,
bowing his head as he took a step closer.

"Thank you," she whispered, genuinely pleased by his
words. Her eyes took on a dreamy tint and her fingers
ached to play in the thick glossy blue-black locks that
brushed the collar of his suit coat. "I, um, I think Sam
needs you," she said then, waving toward her husband's

partner, who stood near the double doors to the conference room.

Ivan sent a quick nod in Sam's direction before turning back to his wife. "I'll see you at home," he told her.

"Zhabi?" she blurted, then glanced around to see if anyone else had heard her. "Um, do you think maybe we could go out tonight? Dinner? A club or take in a show or something? It *is* New Year's Eve," she noted softly.

"Sounds good," Ivan said, reaching for her hand and squeezing it inside his. "I'll call you later and we can talk about it, okay?"

Rencia glowed. "'Kay."

Ivan favored her with a wink and pressed a quick kiss to the back of her hand. Then he left.

"Lawrencia?" someone called.

Rencia couldn't take her eyes from her husband. "Coming," she drawled absently.

Shelby Daniels saluted her friend with a raised glass of champagne. "I can't wait to brag to everyone on my job about my girl's first commercial," she raved.

Hester's dark eyes sparkled as merrily as the white lights and balloons decorating the club. "Thanks Shelby. Damn it, why didn't I leave GeFran sooner? I could've been doing these things so long ago."

Shelby toyed with a long lock of her hair extensions and sighed. "All in good time, right? Maybe this is the way it was supposed to happen."

"Hmph," Hester replied, her expression souring. "That Breeze commercial'll probably hit the screen before mine, damn it."

"Hes, does it really matter?"

"I wouldn't expect you to understand this, Shell."

"Why? Because I work in a bank and not a high-powered cosmetics company? Sweetie, believe me, inexperienced people are chosen for jobs over experienced people in all positions all the time."

Hester rolled her eyes toward the crowded dance floor below. "Geneva and Frank have made as much money off my face and body as they will off that green-eyed bitch they're droolin' over."

Shelby groaned and focused her attention on a loose string clinging to her body-hugging blue dress. "Girl, are you ever gonna let this go?" she groaned.

Something on the dance floor caught Hester's calculating gaze and she sat a bit straighter on the stool she occupied. "No," she replied and left her girlfriend alone at the table.

"Hester?" Shelby called, surprised by the sudden departure. "Hester!"

After dinner at a small Chinese restaurant not far from their home, Ivan and Rencia set out for an evening of club-hopping. They ventured into the Grey Shell, a new but well-known reggae dance hall in Harlem. As they strolled past the long line outside the establishment, someone recognized Rencia and a tiny huddle of admirers gathered to shake hands with the Breeze Girl.

"I didn't know so many brothas read fashion magazines," Ivan noted in a frustrated tone, though his magnificent looks had garnered him just as much attention from the ladies.

Rencia curved her hand into the crease of her husband's powerful arm and leaned close. "Well, you know, a few of my ads have appeared in some of the men's magazines."

Ivan looked down at her. "No, I didn't know."

"Well, that's probably how they recognized me," she explained, oblivious to her husband's aggravation.

"Larry—"

"Oooh, Zhabi, let's dance," she interjected, already excited by the sultry island grooves filling the club.

Ivan rolled his eyes and warned himself to calm down. He acknowledged the fact that his wife could draw a man's attention without even trying, whether she was the Breeze Girl or not. He allowed her to pull him onto the crowded hardwood floor.

The music was slow and brought out the lusty instincts in its listeners. Ivan and Rencia were no exceptions. They held each other in a scandalously seductive embrace, grinding in sync to the beats filling their ears.

"I wanted to tell you something today before I left the office."

"What?" She sighed, lost in the relaxing music.

Ivan slid his mouth closer to her ear. "I like what working for GeFran has done for you."

Rencia smiled and pulled back to fix him with a wicked look. "Yeah, it has done wonders for my bank account," she teased.

Ivan grinned and nodded. "I'm sure it has. Actually, I was referring to you. Your personality."

Rencia feigned offence. "I didn't realize there was anything wrong with it."

"There wasn't," he assured her promptly. "Working for GeFran just added something to it. I never thought you could be more incredible than you already were."

"Zhabi, that's so sweet," Rencia cooed, stroking his flawless fair skin.

Ivan only grimaced. "Don't kiss me yet."

"So there is a 'but' behind this compliment?"

"A small one."

"Spill it."

Ivan took a deep breath and pulled Rencia close again. "I guess I'm still havin' a problem accepting all these changes."

Rencia pressed a light kiss to the corner of his mouth. "Baby, why? You said it yourself how great my working for GeFran has been. We even had an opportunity to work together. I know you never planned on that happening."

"No, and it was great, love," Ivan softly assured her, his hands massaging the silky skin of her back left bare by the daring cut of the black slip dress she wore. "It's just that I had . . . other plans for us."

Confusion marred Rencia's delicate brow. "What type of plans?"

"I'd just wanted us to experience so many things once I got this partnership up and running."

"Things like what?"

The simple question rendered Ivan speechless. He couldn't bring himself to be completely open and tell her that he lived for the day when they would share a child together. Somehow he didn't think she'd welcome the idea in lieu of her blossoming career. Hearing her response to that issue wasn't something he was ready for.

"Zhabi?"

Ivan forced an easy smile to his face. "I'd just planned on being able to spend a lot more time with my luscious wife, that's all. I'm my own boss now and that counts for a lot. Now, your schedule is so hectic—"

Rencia cupped his face in her palms. "Baby, that's what tonight is about. We're just gonna have to steal time and make the most of it. Besides, a new year is coming. We've got to make it better than these past few months."

"Mmm," Ivan grunted, leaning down to press a lingering kiss to her mouth. "I like the sound of that," he murmured with the kiss. When he pulled away, he noticed Rencia took a while to open her eyes. "Was it that good?" he taunted.

"Yes," she confirmed sweetly, though she still appeared drained. "However, I think such a heavy dinner on top of such a long day is catching up with me."

"Let's sit for a while, then we'll get out of here," he suggested, already turning to escort her from the floor.

Rencia offered no arguments as that drained feeling threatened to remove all the strength from her legs. When she heard her name, she groaned and cursed the fact that Ivan hadn't suggested they leave.

"Well, well, if it ain't the Breeze Girl."

"Hester." Rencia sighed, happy that it wasn't another adoring fan. "How are you?"

"Not as good as you. You must be floating on cloud nine," she noted, effectively masking the hate in her dark eyes with a look that was syrupy sweet.

Rencia leaned back against Ivan's chest and shook her head. "Girl, right now I just want to float into a bed."

"Mmm, I can definitely understand that," Hester stated slyly, her wide eyes roaming Ivan's face and incredible frame.

"Oh, I'm sorry," Rencia whispered and glanced at her husband. "Hester Morgan, this is—"

"Ivan, it's nice to see you again," Hester interrupted smoothly, a jolt of glee piercing through her when she glimpsed surprise in Rencia's eyes.

Ivan kept his arms around his wife's body as he nodded. "Same here," he replied.

"I spoke with your partner," Hester went on, her eyes practically devouring Ivan as she spoke. "I'm looking forward to working with the both of you."

"Sam will be glad to hear that," he told her, since his partner had been the one to express such interest over working with Hester.

Hester smoothed her hands across the revealing halter jumpsuit she sported. "Well, I'll let you two get on with your evening. Lawrencia," she added, as though it were an afterthought.

Rencia's light eyes narrowed in suspicion, but before she could voice her concerns, a long yawn overcame her.

"Larry?" Ivan called, amusement tingeing his chiseled features. "You need me to carry you out of here?"

"I will if we don't leave right now."

Ivan pressed his forehead against hers. "Good. I prefer bringing in the new year at home anyway," he remarked in a sly tone, joining Rencia when she laughed.

Ivan normally patronized a small café located in the building where his new firm was located. Each morning, after ordering his usual fix of milk and donuts, he took a seat at his favorite table. One day, he overheard a group of young men talking and he couldn't help but be interested in the topic of discussion. It seemed they were raving over something or someone in a magazine.

"Damn, I tell you she is so hot!" one of the young men drawled.

"Is she black?" one of them asked.

The only African-American male seated at the table spoke up. "Hell yeah, she's black. Can't you tell?" he asked.

One of the other young men took offence. "I couldn't tell. With those green eyes and that hair—"

"Save it, y'all. The Breeze Girl is definitely a sista."

Another one of the young men spoke up. "Damn, what I wouldn't give for a minute alone with her," he said.

That did it for Ivan. He stood from the table, pushing his chair back with such force it almost teetered to the floor. Knowing that if he heard much more of the juvenile rambling, he was liable to snap, he stormed out of the café. He made it to the elevators and was about to step inside when Sam caught him.

"Hey, man, what's the rush? We work for ourselves now, remember?" Sam asked. At the fierce scowl on his partner's face, his own expression grew serious. "What's goin' on?"

Ivan waved his hand in the air. "Man, I'm tryin' like hell to stay in check about Rencia modeling, but it's a lot harder than I thought it'd be," he admitted.

"What happened?" Sam asked.

Ivan shook his head. "These fools in that restaurant downstairs. Talkin' about how fine she is and about what they'd give to have a minute alone with her."

Sam laughed shortly. "Man, she is fine."

Ivan turned his narrowed black stare toward his friend. "I know that, but I don't need every jackass I see reminding me of it."

"Man, think of it as a compliment," Sam advised. "Do you know how many brothas, hell, how many men period would kill to have Rencia by their side?"

"I'd rather not know," Ivan muttered, rolling his eyes to the floor.

Sam sighed and shook his head. "Man, I hope you can keep this attitude to yourself around your wife. This outlook of yours could ruin your marriage."

"Could you chill with the advice, Sam?" Ivan requested firmly.

Sam decided to leave it alone, but the look of concern was still etched on his face.

Ivan sitting about fifteen feet away. A devious smile crossed her lips as she appraised him. There was certainly no denying how strongly he'd always affected her.

The fact that Rencia spent so much time with David Milner had to be a sore spot between them, hence her scheme the previous evening. Hester decided it might be nice to see just how far she could get with Ivan again. Hell, she thought, it would be better than nice. Maybe this time she could get him to do something more. Something that would call for a more private arena. In the process, perhaps she could wipe that graceful smile from Rencia's face.

Smoothing her hands over the skimpy red cocktail dress she wore, Hester sauntered over to Ivan's table. Her eyes lingered on his beautiful black hair, pulled back into a ponytail. He wore a dark denim shirt, jeans, and a pair of black hiking boots. The outfit added even more sexiness to his rugged veneer.

Ivan's eyes were focused on his wife and David Milner laughing and talking across the room. Hester gleefully noted that he was drinking.

"Do you mind some company?" she asked, taking a seat at the small table.

Ivan's obsidian stare slid toward her before returning to the other side of the room. When he shrugged, Hester smiled and began pushing the half-empty gin bottle out of her way.

Watching him with a blatantly seductive smile, she leaned forward. "I didn't know you drank so much, Ivan."

He grimaced and tossed back another shot of the clear alcohol. "I don't."

Hester leaned back in her seat and followed his gaze across the room. "Oh . . . I see," she said, pretending to have just spotted David and Rencia. "You know, I'm sure they're only discussing my layout for *Gentlemen's Corner*. It's coming up soon."

"I'm sure they are too," Ivan conceded, filling another shot glass to the brim.

"But I'm also sure David's loving every minute of it," Hester said. "I'll bet when he found out Rencia was coming to Atlantic City he came up with fifty ways to get time alone with her," she added, watching Ivan's expression grow deadlier.

Suddenly, she snapped her fingers. "I'll bet Rencia didn't fall for that crap though. She was probably tryin' to get as much time alone with you as possible," she commented, knowing Ivan and Rencia had hardly been seen together during the trip.

As she hoped, the statement aggravated Ivan even further. For the next half hour, Hester sat there filling Ivan's head with all sorts of notions regarding Rencia and David Milner. In truth, Ivan knew he was a fool to be taking any of Hester's observations as fact. Unfortunately, the alcohol served as a powerful catalyst, helping the lies consume his mind . . . and his heart.

Rencia and David left the bar arm in arm fifteen minutes later. Ivan slammed his glass to the table. Hester's eyes widened when she saw several cracks marring the smooth sides of the thick glass. Standing from her seat, she walked over to him and placed her arms around his shoulders.

"Honey, let me take you back to your room. I think you've had enough to drink." She smiled when he stood and allowed her to lead him out of the bar.

Rencia said her good-byes to David just outside the elevators on the opposite side of where Ivan and Hester were.

"Look, thanks David. I think Hester's gonna be in good hands."

David shrugged. "Yeah, well, I always aim to please," he assured her, pressing a kiss to her cheek.

When he'd gone, Rencia punched the elevator button, deciding to go on to her room. Just then, her cell phone rang.

"This is Lawrencia," she answered.

"Hi, it's Geneva. Any luck with that handsome husband of yours?"

Rencia leaned against the paneled elevator wall and sighed. "Well, I'm surprised to say I think he just might do it."

"Oh, that's wonderful." Geneva sighed and leaned back against her desk chair. "Lance is practically salivating, he wants you two together so badly."

"Yeah, me too," Rencia admitted, though her words held a completely different meaning.

Geneva smiled. "Even a stranger can see the love and chemistry you two have. It's not something you find every day, and if you have another chance to make things right, you should take it."

Inside Ivan's room, Hester was doing her best to tease and arouse him. Unfortunately for her, it was of no use. She managed to get him undressed, marveling at the awesome build of his body. Ivan, however, had long since dozed off.

"Damn it, to hell!" she hissed, kicking the edge of the king-size bed with the tip of her shoe. "Forget this," she grumbled, preparing to leave.

"Zhabi? Zhabi, you in there?"

Hester heard Rencia calling and her devious mind went to work. Pulling off her skimpy dress, she situated herself and Ivan between the sheets.

Rencia knocked softly, before she pushed open the door connecting the rooms. When she walked in and saw Hester snuggled in Ivan's arms, her body seemed to shut down. She couldn't move or scream or do anything else.

Hester hid the devious smile that threatened to break through. "Oh Lord, Rencia!" she cried, pretending to be flustered. "Ivan didn't tell me you had connecting rooms!" She reached for her dress and panties discarded on the floor.

Rencia was still too shocked to speak, though she did grimace when she saw the comforter fall away to reveal Hester's nude body.

All the moving around and the sound of Hester's voice as she apologized to Rencia roused Ivan from his slumber. His sleek, black brows drew together in a frown when he saw Hester slipping into her clothes. She pulled the dress down over her hips before leaving the bed to slip into her underwear. Ivan winced, sensing they were not alone, and turned his head toward the other side of the room.

Seeing Rencia sent the most intense pain through his stomach. She wasn't hysterical or crying. She only stood watching him. Her eyes were tinged with sadness.

Ivan was still somewhat unclear about what was happening, so there was little he could say. However, things weren't so fuzzy that he couldn't figure out what Rencia must have been thinking.

"Larry—" he began, wincing as the simple act of talking sent shots of pain through his head.

Rencia jerked at the sound of Ivan calling her name. Before he could utter another word, she ran from the room. Not wanting to face Ivan either, Hester left soon after.

In her room, Rencia had already started to pack. Once she'd finished, she planned on calling Geneva to let her know she'd be unable to stay in the same hotel for the duration of the trip.

She'd walked over to the closet to retrieve the last few articles of clothing when Ivan burst through the adjoining door next to it. Rencia flinched, but didn't look at him. Instead, she folded the clothes over her arm and tried to step around him, her eyes downcast.

Ivan took her by the arm. "Larry—"

"Get off me," she replied quietly, wrenching her arm out of his grasp.

Ivan sighed and followed her into the room. Seeing the Louis Vuitton luggage lying open on the bed, he closed his eyes. "Larry, you have to let me explain."

Rencia shrugged. "Nothin' to explain. I was there, remember?"

"I know what you saw," he began, running one hand through his thick hair. "But it wasn't what—it wasn't—"

"Wasn't what, Ivan?" She turned on him. "What? It wasn't you and Hester in bed together? Is that what it wasn't?"

Ivan tried to calm down before he spoke. "Baby, I swear I don't know how I got there," he whispered.

Rencia's mouth fell open in surprise. "Ivan, please! You must think I'm a damn idiot!"

"I don't think that, Larry," he assured her, taking a step closer.

"Get out."

"Larry—"

"I *said* get out!" she exploded, pushing against his heavily muscled bare chest. He didn't budge and she stopped pushing and began to hit him.

Ivan let her vent her anger, bringing his arms around her when she collapsed against him and started to cry.

"How could you do this now?" she whispered in a weak voice.

Ivan buried his face in her hair. "I didn't have sex with her."

Rencia pushed herself away from him. "Will you stop tellin' me that? I saw you!"

"Larry, I know what you saw, but it didn't happen."

Rencia raised her hand as a signal for him to stop. "I have to get out of here."

"Doin' what you do best, huh, Larry?"

Rencia turned to face him, her perfectly arched brows rising slightly. "Excuse me?"

Ivan shrugged and pushed one hand into the deep pockets of his saggy jeans. "Instead of standing here talking about this, you're ready to leave."

"Standing here? I can't believe you have the nerve to stand here trying to get me to believe nothing happened in that room, when I saw you in bed with the bitch!"

"Just so you know, she approached me in the bar where I was having a drink alone while you were laughin' it up with David Milner, as usual."

"What?" Rencia hissed, thoroughly confused.

"Don't even try it. Ever since we got here the two of you have been all up under each other."

"It's been business! For Hester! Can you believe it?"

"Business," Ivan muttered. "Probably the business of when and where he'll finally get to take you to bed."

Rencia's expression sharpened. "To hell with you."

"Mmm . . . I'm sure Milner would definitely approve of that."

"I can't believe this," Rencia said, as though she were speaking to herself. "I can't believe we're talking about me and David when it was you and Hester in bed!"

Ivan winced and looked away for a moment. "Larry, do you even recall that she had her shoes on when she left my bed?"

A devilish smirk crossed Rencia's mouth. "You seem to like it that way."

"Damn!" he bellowed, losing what little control he had left over his temper. "Listen, believe whatever the hell you want to. I'm through with this mess. If you want to go, go. Go!"

Rencia marched over to the bed and closed the case. "For your information, I'm not leaving, just going to another hotel."

"Well, I guess that'll make Milner's night," Ivan said, delivering the parting shot. He watched as Rencia paused in the doorway before she left.

Chapter Nineteen

After that night, Rencia did her best to avoid Ivan during GeFran and Destiny negotiations. It was difficult, considering the things Ivan had said to her about David and what happened with Hester, but she managed.

Lance Margolis was all smiles when Rencia arrived for the Breeze shoot. The elaborate loft studio located in the heart of the garment district was rumored to be where Lance held his most shocking photo sessions. Despite the rainy, cold, overcast conditions outside, the studio was warm and scented with the most aromatic candles.

Rencia arrived with her face scrubbed free of makeup and her silky curls piled into a high ponytail. Her green eyes, though always vibrant, were tinged with a sadness impossible to miss.

"Right on time, as usual," Lance drawled, squeezing Rencia's hands as he bestowed a kiss to both her cheeks.

"Sorry about Ivan, Lance."

"Hmm?"

"I'm sorry I couldn't convince him to do this," she clarified, unbuttoning the chic cashmere swing coat she sported. "I'm confident, though, that I can give you what you want with whomever you've chosen to work opposite me."

Lance listened as Rencia rambled on. He led her through the maze of hallways to the corridor of lavish dressing rooms.

"Go on and change out of your clothes and into the lounging gown inside the closet," Lance instructed, as he guided her past the doorway. "Makeup will be here in a moment."

Rencia nodded, though she barely heard Lance. Her thoughts were so jumbled and she prayed her frustration would not come through in her work. For a moment, she braced her hands on the oak countertop and bowed her head. Then, forcing herself to focus on business, she pulled the barrette from her ponytail and let her hair cascade past her shoulders. When she looked up into the mirrors, she saw Ivan behind her.

"You," she breathed, turning to find him lounging in the room's living area. "What are you doing here?"

Ivan kept his dark eyes trained on the newspaper he studied. "Didn't you ask me to be here?"

"Yes, but I, I thought—"

"What?"

Rencia pushed herself from the counter. "I didn't think you'd agree to it . . . after what happened."

"Nothing happened, Larry. I told you that."

"How could you have expected me to believe that so easily?"

"Because I'm telling you the truth."

Rencia watched him, growing angrier at his impossibly cool attitude. "What kind of game are you playing?"

Ivan set his paper aside and stood. Rencia's eyes were inexorably drawn to his sleek, bare chest visible beneath a gauzy, ankle-length white robe and matching pajama pants that hung low across his lean waist.

"No game, Larry. This is about the business, and if it

will benefit by having me participate in this shoot, then so be it."

"Bull."

Ivan smiled, though his expression was not humorous. He bowed his head and walked slowly toward her. "I don't know, Larry. I guess this is my chance to see if you really are the professional everyone boasts you are. Or maybe you're just a beauty with no real head for business, a pretty face who wears her heart on her sleeve."

Rencia ordered herself not to blink as she glared up at her husband's face. She knew he was trying to goad her and refused to allow him the pleasure. Instead, she turned and sauntered to the dressing room door. Luckily, one of the photographer's staff was on his way past.

"Excuse me," she called, smiling at the young man who watched her in awe. "Would you please tell Mr. Margolis that we're ready to get this thing started?"

"All right, you two. As you can see, I've cleared the room. I want to make this the most comfortable experience possible."

Hmph, Rencia thought, *you'd have a better chance of getting a pit bull to work with a kitten.*

"Now," Lance continued, "the concept for the shoot is a love scene. A simple premise that should be a piece of cake for the two of you, because you're comfortable making love to one another."

"What?" Rencia blurted, from her spot behind Lance's desk.

Lance chuckled, as did Ivan.

"Oh. Ren, love, I don't really expect you to make love. Just a little light foreplay."

The explanation did little to console Rencia. She fiddled with the graceful folds of her lounging gown and tried to keep her eyes away from the wolfish grin spreading across Ivan's face.

"Now, if you'll follow me," Lance instructed, as he led them from his office and into a larger adjoining room.

Rencia felt her heart bouncing around in her stomach when she looked upon the exquisite setting. Soft jazz vibrated from overhead speakers, and the room was furnished with a huge black sofa and a matching armchair next to a round glass end table that supported glasses and a silver bucket with a champagne bottle chilling inside. The corner window offered a soothing view of the freezing rain streaming down the panes. In contrast, a fan provided a cool breeze against the white, floor-length drapes. The most spectacular prop in the room, though, had to be the magnificent round bed that was set with a milky white comforter, crisp white linens, and fluffy pillows.

"Okay now, the two of you get comfortable on the chair," Lance called, as he went to change to his lenses. "Rencia, sit on Ivan's lap."

Rencia's lashes fluttered, but she stifled her uneasiness and told herself that this was business. Pleasure was not on the agenda, despite the fact that she was working with a man who could make her melt with a simple touch, word, or look.

"Larry?" Ivan called. He seemed right at home in the overstuffed armchair. Though he appeared cool enough, his entrancing stare was extraordinarily intense as it raked her lovely hair flowing to her waist and the seductive, practically transparent gown.

Rencia stepped closer and was about to take her place. Suddenly, Ivan squeezed her wrist.

"Here, straddle my lap," he suggested, his big hands already moving to her hips to position her accordingly.

Rencia didn't argue, praying that if she offered her full cooperation, the shoot would end that much sooner. Of course, nothing prepared her for the scandalous tingle ignited within her when she touched Ivan's body.

"You okay?" he whispered, knowing how he was affecting her.

"Mmm-hmm," she managed, keeping her face averted and her head bowed.

"Larry?"

"I'm fine, Zhabi, all right?" she hissed.

"Larry, you know what you saw in Atlantic City was a lie."

"Everyone always told me Hester wanted you."

"Do you believe I wanted her?" he asked, his expression probing. "I pray you don't, Larry. I haven't wanted another woman since the first time I saw you."

Rencia's slender fingers curled around the lapels of Ivan's robe. She melted against him.

"All right, you two, we're finally ready to get this thing going. Oh, good, good, I like the straddling," Lance raved, as he aimed the camera from its tripod. "Now, I'm going to just begin shooting and you guys do what you feel. Rencia, I want to give Ivan a bit more control here. I'll call out to him when I want you to change positions."

Rencia barely nodded as she forced her eyes back to Ivan's.

"I love you," he mouthed while leaning close. His hands massaged her thighs through her robe as his lips traveled the line of her jaw. Rencia's fingers weakened against his chest as she leaned into the whisper-soft kiss.

"Very nice," Lance interjected smoothly. "*Very* nice."

The soft, methodic clicks of the camera shutter filled

the studio as the scene progressed. Ivan settled his arms around Rencia's waist. One of his hands moved upward to stroke her back. The other cupped her breast so briefly she thought she'd imagined it.

"Zhabi." She gasped softly, when his hand curved around her thigh, allowing his lips more room to explore the silky column of her neck. Tentatively, her fingers ventured beneath the robe and she trailed the outline of his rigid pecs and abs.

"Wonderful, completely sensual," Lance continued to rave. "Ivan, I want you to ease out of the chair, taking Lawrencia with you to the sofa."

Rencia almost whimpered when she heard the request. She feared Lance's sensual photo shoot was about to become something much more erotic.

Ivan stood effortlessly, taking Rencia across the short space to the sofa. She pushed the robe from his shoulders and massaged his arms as he laid her flat and settled his considerable weight against her. Again, his hands roamed her thighs, settling beneath her full derriere as he lifted her into his semihard arousal. Rencia heard his muffled groan when their bodies touched. His tongue traced the pulse at the base of her throat before trailing her collarbone and the swell of her bosom above the loose bodice of the gown.

"Perfect," Lance inserted softly amidst the clicking shudders.

Rencia wound her arms about Ivan's neck and played in his hair. She arched herself into his unyielding frame and moaned unashamedly when his nose outlined the valley between her breasts.

"Yes!" Lance cried, knowing he was creating a masterpiece. He moved around the studio at a frantic pace, bent on capturing every alluring angle of the entrancing couple. "Take her to the bed."

Ivan was the perfect subject. He gave Lance everything he asked for and more. Of course, the fact that he was working with his lovely wife on one of the most enjoyable of tasks was his motivation.

For the third time that afternoon, Ivan found Rencia's thighs irresistible. This time, his hands disappeared beneath the folds of the gown and he parted her legs in order to settle himself between them.

"Ivan," Rencia whispered in a warning tone, her eyes widening when she felt the shocking power of his manhood against the center of her body.

"Shh," he urged. His mouth covered hers as his tongue thrust deep past her lips while he rubbed against her like a familiar lover.

"Mmm," she moaned, trembling as she mimicked the slow lunges he pleasured her with.

Ivan's hands moved to her hair and massaged her scalp with languorous strokes. He continued to kiss Rencia with unrestrained passion, until his own needs got the better of him and he had to break the kiss.

"Incredible!" Lance called out, as if on cue. "I want to get a few more shots," he told his subjects, while rushing to the opposite end of the studio. "I need to get something from my office. You two, take five."

Alone in the studio, Ivan and Rencia were too exhausted by unsatisfied passion to speak one word.

The session only lasted another forty minutes, but it seemed like a lifetime to the DeZhabis.

"I can't wait to get inside the darkroom," Lance went on, as he had for the last several minutes. "Rencia, you were ravishing as always. Ivan, if you ever think about changing careers, give me a call."

"Thanks, Lance," Ivan replied, enjoying the well-known photographer's compliments far more than he realized.

Rencia ran shaking fingers across her brow and fixed Ivan with a scathing look. "I hope you enjoyed that," she told him once they were alone.

Ivan slipped back into his robe. "Oh, believe me, I did," he confirmed, smiling when her eyes narrowed in disgust. When she whirled away and stormed out of the studio, he allowed the smile to fade. With a determined glint in his deep gaze, he headed over to a black wall phone and dialed the necessary digits.

"Good afternoon. Louis Davis, please."

Chapter Twenty

"What a shady bitch." Casey surmised three weeks later when Rencia invited her for Thanksgiving and told her about Hester Morgan's betrayal over dinner that evening.

"Mmm," she replied, staring across the room out the window offering its view of the late evening New Jersey sky. The arrival of November brought fresh snow to the city. It clung to the corners of the windows, giving them a frosty allure.

"I can't believe you didn't kick her rank behind out the room," Casey said.

"Hell, Case, I couldn't even move. It was like I was paralyzed or something," Rencia said, shaking her head.

Casey reached across the table and patted her hand. "I know, girl."

"Anyway," Rencia announced, leaving her chair, "it's over and I guess it's all for the best. Maybe it wasn't meant to last between Ivan and me."

"You don't believe that," Casey detected. "I know Ivy doesn't think that."

Rencia winced at the sound of her husband's name. "How is he?"

Casey sighed and stood as well. "Girl, I can't even begin to describe how badly he's doing. He won't talk to anyone, he hardly eats. It's like he's in a trance or something."

Frustrated, Rencia pushed her hands through her hair. "God, it was so hard tryin' to work through all the problems in our marriage. Problems we still haven't solved, and now this mess." She stared blankly past the windows.

Casey clasped her hands together and stepped closer to her friend. "Honey, do you really think Ivan had sex with her?"

"At first I did," Rencia admitted, turning toward Casey. "But I know he'd never do that. Not when we'd been so close."

"Then, baby, please tell Ivan that. Tell him something. It could probably start working out some of this mess."

Rencia fixed Casey with a rueful smile. "You're right. We do need to talk, but I don't think I know where to start."

Casey decided there was nothing more to say. "Girl, I better be getting back before it gets any later," she said, strolling toward the stairs to get her coat from the bedroom.

Rencia was about to head back to the kitchen, where she'd been doing dishes, when her intercom buzzer sounded.

"Yeah, Mike?" she answered after pressing the button.

Mike's voice was just above a whisper. "Hey, Rencia, listen I've got two big guys down here at the front desk claiming to be your brothers."

Rencia could barely hold back a happy scream at the security guard's announcement. "It's okay! Send 'em up!" she shouted into the intercom's receiver.

A few moments later, Casey arrived downstairs. "All

right, Ren, I'm outta here," she said just as the doorbell sounded. "I got it."

Casey pulled open the door and almost collided with what could have easily been mistaken for a wall. "Lennon?" she breathed, her eyes widening in disbelief as she gazed up at the huge dark man.

Lennon Davis smiled, enjoying the shocked expression on Casey's beautiful face. Stepping closer, he grabbed her tiny waist and pulled her into a hug.

Casey instantly softened against the man she'd had a crush on since their meeting at Ivan and Rencia's wedding.

Lennon gave her a sexy wink and tugged at her coat. "I hope you're not leavin'?"

Casey's heart fluttered madly in her chest at the sound of his baritone voice. Still, she managed to maintain her composure. "Uh . . . I was," she stammered.

"Stay awhile," Lennon urged, moving her back inside the condo.

"All right," Casey agreed, barely able to keep herself from staring wantonly at Lennon's captivating dark features.

"Happy Thanksgiving, Case!"

"Hey, Louie," Casey said, hugging Rencia's next oldest and equally handsome brother.

Rencia stood in the center of the living room, waiting for her hugs and kisses. Lennon had other ideas.

"What the hell is goin' on with you and Ivan?" he said the moment he spotted her across the room.

Louis followed suit. "Yeah, Ren, don't you think this separation crap has gone on long enough?"

Rencia's sleek brows drew closed to form a frown. "This seperation crap is none of your business."

"Well, are you gonna talk this out or what?" Lennon's gaze was furious.

"Yes," Rencia replied sharply.

"When?"

"None of your business!"

"How are y'all gonna work out anything with Ivan in Brooklyn and you in Jersey?" Louis questioned, laying his navy bomber jacket across the sofa.

Rencia squeezed her eyes shut. "Will you two please stay out of my business? I'll go see Ivan when the time is right."

"When is that?" Lennon asked, not put off by her attitude.

When I get up the nerve, Rencia told herself, shaking her head at her two overbearing yet well-meaning brothers. "Will you two please come over here and hug me?" She sighed, losing her interest in arguing.

The two, brooding young men forgot their anger for a moment. They walked over to their baby sister, and the three embraced for a long while.

"Believe it or not, we didn't come out here to jump down your throat."

Rencia's smile was playfully suspicious as she looked up at Lennon. "I *don't* believe it, but humor me anyway. Why are you here? For a bit of turkey and dressing? Somehow I don't think that's it."

Lennon went to put up his coat, while Louis escorted his sister to the sofa. "Pop wants to take us on some kind of trip for the holidays."

"A trip?"

"Yeah, said he thought we could all use some time away," Louis explained.

"Hmph, I think he just wants to baby Curl, Lennon

said, referring to his sister. "Spoil her more than she already is."

Rencia grabbed a pillow and threw it at Lennon. "It sounds like a great idea. I could use a getaway, especially now."

Louis's stare was probing. "You don't have any photo sessions or anything else planned?"

Rencia hesitated before answering. She thought of Ivan's invitation to his parents anniversary party in London. As badly as she wanted to see her in-laws for the new year, she didn't think she was ready for the onslaught of emotions sure to rise once she saw her husband.

"I have nothing planned," she told her brothers. "The sooner we leave, the better."

Rencia decided to turn in a while later. She left Lennon, Louis, and Casey downstairs to chat the night away. Louis left the dining room to raid the refrigerator for Thanksgiving leftovers, giving Lennon and Casey a moment alone.

"So what's been up, Case?"

Casey shrugged and leaned back in her chair. "Nothin' much. Just livin'."

Lennon's dark eyes narrowed slightly. "I'd say life's treating you well," he surmised.

Casey felt a slight chill shimmy up her spine, but maintained her regal composure. "I can't complain."

As Lennon watched her, he couldn't believe how difficult it was for him to look away. She had always been lovely, but now there was something more. He always felt Casey was far too young for him. She's just turned thirty-one and he would be turning forty in another year. They had nothing in common, but seeing her then made him question that. Her sensuality seemed to reach out to him like a tangible thing.

"So what's up?" he asked, more suggestively this time.

"You asked me that already."

"You know what I mean."

Louis returned to the living room just then and the conversation smoothly returned to Ivan and Rencia.

"So Ivy *did* set this up?" Casey sighed, once the brothers told her what was really going on.

"He knew Curl would back out, so he asked us to make sure she was there," Lennon explained.

"I think they need this time together," Casey decided.

Louis shrugged. "Hell yeah, they do, but we all know they won't make the effort." He watched his brother nod in agreement.

Casey sighed. "Good luck with this, guys."

"What do you mean 'guys'?" Lennon bellowed. "You're comin' with us."

"Me? Why?" Casey shrieked.

"They *are* your family, Case," Louis interjected.

"But—"

"I want you there," Lennon added. His expression was serious when Casey turned to look at him.

"This is a nice thing you all are doing," Casey admitted, shaking off the shiver Lennon's eyes cast upon her. "But Ivy and Rencia have been trying to get back together for how long now? Even the joy of the holiday season in a romantic place like London may not be enough for those two. It's like so much mess is keeping them from taking a chance on each other again."

Lennon stretched his long legs across the sofa and leaned his head back. "Well, maybe we need a backup plan."

"Such as?" Louis asked.

"We should do something together as a family—the younger crowd, you know? After New Year's. Get away for a weekend or some crap like that."

Louis rolled his eyes toward his brother. "A weekend? This is Ivan and Rencia, remember?"

Lennon chuckled softly. "Yeah, maybe a week."

Casey laughed. "That's a start. Maybe we could get them up there under the ruse that it's a family thing, then leave 'em alone, without family, phones, the pressures of their careers."

Lennon and Louis both nodded.

"Not bad, Case, not bad at all," Lennon said.

Casey was pleased with the idea, but prayed it wouldn't be necessary. Perhaps the trip to London would be enough of a catalyst to help her cousin and her friend repair their marriage.

Chapter Twenty-one

"You people have conspired one time too many where my marriage is concerned and I've let you get away with it. Daddy, I would've expected something like this out of Len, Lou, and Casey. But you?"

Rencia rambled on as her family walked ahead of her. She'd been going on for hours, it seemed. Ever since they arrived at JFK and she realized they were traveling to London.

Lawrence Davis slowed his steps and allowed his sons, his daughter-in-law, and Casey to lead the way to Heathrow's baggage area. His arm settled around his daughter's shoulders as he squeezed her against his taller frame.

"Baby, you know that I've always tried to stay out of you kids' personal affairs, but Ivan asked for our help himself. I couldn't see turning down my son-in-law."

"But *I'm* your daughter. No disrespect, Daddy, but you don't know everything that's going on in our relationship."

"That's very true," Lawrence admitted, his salt-and-pepper mustache twitching when he smiled. "Ivan knows, though. This is obviously his way of getting some time alone with you away from the pressures of your lives in New York."

Rencia's jade stare clouded with sadness. "We've had time away before," she told her father, remembering the weeks spent in Louisiana before the situation took a turn for the worse. "It didn't seem to help us much."

Lawrence stopped walking and faced his daughter. "You know what might help?" he asked, cupping her face in his big hands. "Lower your expectations. Don't expect every meeting between the two of you to be used for heavy conversations. It's Christmastime. Enjoy it."

"That would be nice."

"Think you could give it a shot?"

Rencia could offer no response. Instead, she pulled her father close and hugged him tightly. Lawrence patted her cheek, then went off to help the others collect the bags. Rencia lagged behind, wondering what the week would bring.

"Excuse me, could I get your autograph?"

Rencia closed her eyes, in no mood to entertain a fan. Still, she forced a smile to her face and turned. "Zhabi?" she said when she looked up into her husband's handsome face.

"Merry Christmas," he said, his voice light and melodic.

Rencia slapped her gloved hands to her sides. "Congratulations. Your scheme was successful."

Ivan reached for her hand and pressed it to his chest. Despite the thickness of his gray bomber jacket and matching hooded fleece sweatshirt, Rencia thought she could feel his heart pounding.

"I didn't intend to scheme. It's just that after the shoot and the Hester incident, I got the feeling you'd changed your mind about coming."

Rencia couldn't mask the guilt in her eyes. "You know

me so well," she admitted, looking down as scenes from the erotic photo session filled her memory.

Ivan cupped her chin and forced her to face him. "No better than you know me."

Rencia smiled, reaching up to stroke the back of her gloved hand across his cheek.

"Ivan!"

The moment was interrupted by Lennon's booming voice. After a round of handshakes and hugs, the group headed outside the busy airport and into the snowy night.

Mikende and Anata DeZhabi lived twenty minutes outside London. Crossing the snow-covered stone bridge into their borough was like traveling back in time. While every home boasted a rugged sport-utility or luxury vehicle, the winding roads carried an array of handsome carriages. Two, four, or, in some cases, six people filled the stately engraved buggies that pulled them through snowy streets lit by festive lights that marked the Christmas season.

The main street boasted three pubs. Each appeared equally warm and inviting with glowing candles filling the frost-trimmed windows. Street-side markets sold everything from microwave dinners to homemade soap. Lamppost lights lit every road as far as the eye could see.

"This looks like something right out of a Charles Dickens novel," Casey whispered, her eyes gleaming like a small child's as she gazed out the back window of Ivan's Hummer.

Rencia only nodded, just as captivated by the wintry wonderland as her friend.

"We're here," Ivan announced some time later.

Everyone looked on as the rugged vehicle went up the steep driveway. Massive trees towered overhead, their limbs cluttered with ice and freshly fallen snow. At the crest of the wide gravel drive, the DeZhabi home came into view.

"Trust Aunt Nat to have the place decked out all festive."

"Mmm," Rencia replied, agreeing with Casey's observation as she took in the inviting appearance of the breathtaking estate. Nestled among a smattering of trees, the dark brick home looked as though it had jumped off the pages of a greeting card. Chimneys on either side of the house exuded dark clouds of smoke from their tops, and the massive picture window on the lower level offered a superb view of a gorgeous ten-foot tree.

Ivan backed the Hummer into the five-car garage and popped open the rear entrance. The ladies exited while the men unpacked the trunk.

"How are my girls?" Anata DeZhabi cried, as she rushed toward Rencia and Casey with outstretched arms.

The two young woman squealed with delight as they savored the warm hug. Once Rencia had introduced her mother-in-law to Louis's wife, DeShawn, and Casey had raved over her aunt's dreamy home, Anata pulled Rencia aside and hugged her again.

"We'll talk later, yes?" Anata urged, her expressive almond-shaped gaze expectant.

Rencia smiled and nodded at the request.

"Ivan's missed you, you know?"

Rencia laughed as she nodded. "I know. I've missed him too."

Anata's face, so smooth and radiant it made her appear as youthful as a twenty-year-old, beamed when she heard

Rencia's admission. Without another word, Anata left her daughter-in-law's side and went to greet the others.

Anata had prepared a light, informal meal for her guests' first night in London. Everyone had been urged to serve themselves when hunger struck. Of course, it was impossible to resist the delightful aromas filling the house. A hearty vegetable stew, seasoned and simmered to perfection, homemade pan bread, and hot cider provided a satisfying coat to everyone's stomachs.

"Larry?" Ivan called, when he found his wife in their bedroom. She had ventured over to the enclosed balcony and dined there while enjoying the snowy view of the perfectly landscaped back lawn.

"You mind some company?" he asked, when she smiled up at him.

"Course not, since it looks like we're sharing a room," she said, waving toward the opposite area of the round table.

Ivan's sleek brows rose a few notches. "Mama's not very subtle, is she?"

Rencia shook her head. "I don't mind."

"How's the cider?" Ivan asked, when he settled into his chair.

Rencia giggled and folded her hands around the warm mug. "Perfect. Quite a coincidence, your mother preparing this tonight," she observed knowingly.

Ivan focused on his stew, but couldn't hide his dimpled grin. "I may've mentioned somethin' to her about it."

"Oh, you *may have?*" Rencia taunted, her giggles returning. "Thanks, Zhabi," she whispered, her gaze soft and lingering.

Ivan shrugged slowly. "I was hoping it would remind you of Louisiana."

"It did. The good and the not so good," she admitted,

hoping he understood her meaning. When his expression softened even more, she knew he had.

Ivan cleared his throat and reminded himself of the topic he'd come to discuss. "Larry, um, I don't want to bring up any sore subjects," he began, setting aside his spoon as he spoke. "But I need to tell you how sorry I am about the photo shoot."

"Sorry?" Rencia queried, her brows drawing closed.

"If I humiliated you there," he clarified, leaning back in his chair. "In spite of wanting to please Lance, I think I let myself get carried away. I actually allowed myself to pretend we were okay, that all our problems were solved and we were happy."

"Zhabi," Rencia croaked, feeling her throat constrict as she reached for his hand.

Just then, flickering light in the distance drew their attention. A flurry of children on sleds had taken to the snow for an evening of fun. Although they were far away, the unmistakable lilt of their laughter could still be heard. Rencia felt Ivan's hand tighten around hers. Slowly she squeezed back.

Much later that evening, Lawrence Davis had gone out with a few colleagues who had recently moved to the UK. Once all bags had been unpacked and everyone had eaten, the rest of the group met in the front room for a round of Christmas carols.

Anata and Mikende DeZhabi shared a cozy spot before the fire. They sat on a luxurious black throw rug with Lennon and Casey. Louis and DeShawn shared one of the long sofas, and Ivan and Rencia cuddled close on the other.

Rencia smiled and snuggled back against her husband's wide chest. For the first time since they had separated, she felt a sense of hope. The sound of laughing children had not caused another wave of tension to rise between them. Moreover, it seemed to weave an invisible thread that was slowly binding them together. Perhaps they were on their way back to one another after all.

Lawrencia eyed the gorgeous horse-drawn carriage and the uniformed driver who waited to help her up to the cushioned rear seat.

"You can't be serious about this."

Ivan shrugged. "What's the problem?"

Rencia gestured around her. "It's freezing out here, snow's falling—"

"That's why the carriage ride is better." Ivan argued. "It's safer than driving."

"That Hummer looks pretty rugged," she noted.

Ivan nodded toward the man and decided to escort his wife. "Come on, Larry," he urged, rubbing his gloved hands over her arms. "By the time we get to the pub, everyone will be ready to leave."

Finally, Rencia tugged on the tassels dangling from her yellow knit cap and sighed. "Let's go."

In seconds, they were snuggled inside the buggy with a cashmere blanket tucked around them. The night was especially wintry. Fresh snow had started to fall earlier that day and it quickly sprinkled the sides of the buggy and their clothes.

Ivan glanced toward Rencia and smiled at the wonderment he saw on her face. "Havin' fun?" he murmured against her ear.

"Carriage riding does have its advantages," she admitted, leaning into his shoulder.

"Such as?"

Rencia shrugged and glanced down at the yellow mittens covering her hands. "Well, you can do other things and not have to worry about keeping your eyes on the road."

"Mmm-hmm," he acknowledged, dropping an arm around her shoulders. "What kinds of things?"

"Mmm . . . read the paper, kiss, gaze out at the scenery—"

"What was that second one?"

Rencia pretended to concentrate. "Kiss?"

Ivan nodded. "That's the one," he whispered, his thumbs brushing her chin as he tilted her head back.

Rencia's lashes settled over her eyes as Ivan's lips brushed hers once, then twice. Slowly, his tongue outlined the lush curve of her lips, which parted in anticipation. Instead, he slid his mouth along her jaw and beneath her ear.

"Zhabi . . ." she moaned, cupping his face to bring his lips back to hers. Their mouths met, sweetly at first, then with increased fire as their tongues dueled with maddeningly slow seductiveness.

The elder DeZhabis and Lawrence Davis had opted for an evening in London. The younger crowd decided to stay closer to home and spend their time at one of the local pubs. Mikende suggested the Cocoa Lover, which was owned and operated by a family of fellow restaurateurs.

"I never thought I'd be walking into a British pub owned by black folks," Lennon noted in his booming tone. Of course, he'd only said what everyone else had been thinking.

"I think it's great," Rencia said, taking in the cozy,

friendly atmosphere. Everywhere, people were laughing, proposing toasts, dancing, or eating.

"Shall we?" Louis asked DeShawn. The couple headed for the dance floor.

"I think I saw a pool table upstairs," Casey mentioned, her arched brows rising in a challenging manner as she looked at Lennon.

"Twenty bucks says I can take you," he wagered proudly.

Casey stood. "Ah, surely we can find something more fun to bet on," she taunted and sauntered away with Lennon not far behind.

Ivan rested his arm along the back of the booth and tugged on the low ponytail he sported. "Did you know they were hung up on each other like that?"

Rencia scooped the foamy head off her beer as she nodded. "Yeah, ever since our wedding, they've been ga-ga over each other. I'm glad they're finally doin' something about it."

"Hmph," Ivan grunted, his deep-set eyes gazing off into space. "Seems like a lifetime ago."

"What does?"

"Our wedding."

"Yeah." Rencia sighed as she too recalled that day. "I can't even remember the last time we celebrated our anniversary."

"That Louisiana trip was like magic before—"

"The poem," Rencia finished.

"Yeah." Ivan sighed, looking away. "Larry—"

"I know, Zhabi," Rencia assured him with a soft smile. "Louisiana was an incredible experience, but I think it could have been even more incredible had things been different between us."

Ivan traced the small, heart-shaped necklace Rencia

wore. "I love you," he whispered, tapping his index finger against the base of her throat. "In spite of everything, all the twists and turns our relationship has been through, I never stopped loving you."

"I know that too, Zhabi," she whispered, capturing his finger in her hand. "I know it because I never stopped loving you either."

Each day spent in London was better than the one before. Ivan and Rencia indulged in all the excitement the city had to offer. They shared several more carriage rides, private dinners, and brunches on their bedroom balcony.

Somehow, Ivan managed to keep his distance when the moment rose for more intimate delights. He acknowledged the fact that there were certain topics they'd avoided during their time together. He wanted Rencia desperately, though, and prayed she would come to him.

That weekend, Mikende and Anata DeZhabi celebrated their forty-fourth wedding anniversary. The entire borough had been invited in addition to employees of Mikende's London restaurant and other close friends. It seemed every guest decided to attend.

Once the cake was cut, Mikende and his wife danced to Earth, Wind, and Fire's "Reasons" sung by the Cocoa Lover's house band. The spirit of the evening was contagious. Everyone enjoyed the spectacular spread of food, drink, and music.

Much later, Rencia decided to take a breather. She pulled a black wool wrap over her black, spaghetti-strapped evening gown and took a seat on the back porch swing. She hadn't been there very long when Anata found her.

"Too much for you in there, child?" she teased, settling next to her daughter-in-law.

Rencia shook her head and reached for Anata's hand. "It's wonderful, almost too wonderful. I just wanted to take a few moments and enjoy the snow," she said.

Anata chuckled. "Well, love, I'm almost certain New York will get snow shortly, if they have not already."

The light dulled a bit in Rencia's eyes. "Yeah, but it won't be the same. Everything back there is so frantic and shallow. Here it's so easy and magical."

Anata nudged her shoulder. "Magic can be anywhere you make it."

"Yeah, well, in spite of my uncertainty about this trip, I am regretting having to leave in a couple of days."

"Well, why can't you take some of the magic with you?"

Rencia toyed with a curl dangling from her updo. "I just don't think it would be that simple."

"I don't see why not," Anata argued, her dark almond-shaped gaze expressing optimism. "Lawrencia, I've watched you and Ivan these last days. I've seen the love, the desire. What more do you need?"

Despite the heavy wool covering her skin, Rencia shivered. "I need us to stay here," she said. "Once we get back to New York, I just don't know."

"Why can't the two of you forget all that?"

"What?" Rencia whispered, her eyes narrowing.

Anata waved her small hand in the air. "Forget what has passed. A new year is coming, put all that old baggage behind you and start fresh."

Realization slowly dawned in Rencia's eyes. "My God, you don't know, do you? I can't believe he didn't tell you after all this time."

"Tell me what, child?"

Rencia closed her eyes, then opened them and fixed her mother-in-law with a steady look. "I had a miscarriage. I never even knew I was pregnant. Ivan blamed my career, he blamed me."

Anata was stunned. She clasped her hands together and seemed to utter a silent prayer. "I don't know what to say," she whispered finally.

Rencia kissed her mother-in-law's smooth brown cheek. "There's nothing to say. It was a long time ago."

"But it still keeps the two of you apart?"

"It shouldn't, after all this time, but . . ."

"Have you both sat down and discussed it?"

Rencia shrugged. "We've tried. It always ends in an argument. The last time, I said something I didn't mean. I never knew how set he was on us starting a family. When things began to take off with my career and what happened with the baby, it was like he was a different man. I was different too."

Anata patted Rencia's knee. "You didn't want another child?"

Rencia shook her head. "But not for the reason I let Zhabi believe."

Anata pressed her hand to Rencia's mouth. "Then say no more to me, child. You should finish this talk with your husband. There may be reasons about why he reacted the way he did, that he kept secret as well," Anata said, feeling it best she not share the story of her own miscarriage and the way it affected Ivan.

"I'm afraid to approach the subject again," Rencia admitted. "But I know we can't keep avoiding it."

"I think you'll know when the time is right."

Rencia hugged Anata tightly. She feared that time would never come.

* * *

"I thought I'd find you up here," Ivan called, when he leaned against the bedroom doorjamb.

Rencia closed the closet door. "I was just hanging my wrap. I took a walk earlier."

Ivan met her a few feet from the doorway. "You ready to go back down to the party?" he asked, settling his strong arms around her tiny waist.

"Um, Zhabi," she whispered, leaning past him to push the door closed. "Do you think we could stay up here for a while?" she asked, deciding to take Anata's advice.

The closed door bathed the room in darkness, so Ivan couldn't see the wariness on his wife's face. "No problem with me," he said in a suggestive tone.

"Good, because I really need some time alone with you."

"All you had to do was ask," he whispered, his wide hands encircling her upper arms as his mouth lowered to her neck.

"Zhabi," she breathed, realizing where his thoughts were focused. Lightly, she pressed her palms against the front of his tux.

"Mmm-hmm?" he replied, his hair brushing her skin as his mouth glided across her collarbone. His fingers strummed an imaginary tune against the small of her back, before they ventured higher.

"Wait, Zhabi," she urged, when she felt the straps being lowered on her dress. When the crisp material of Ivan's black tux brushed her bare nipple, she trembled.

Too much time had already passed and Ivan was set on enjoying his wife. He tugged on her arms, silently instructing her to pull them from the straps of her dress.

The gown's clinging material was then peeled down her body, leaving her in a pair of lacy black panties.

Ivan bowed his head, his lips caressing the lush swell and curve of one breast while his hand fondled the other. His tongue traced the nipple, which instantly firmed. A sharp gasp left Rencia's lips, and her need, which had remained dormant, ignited with fierce passion. She threaded her fingers into Ivan's hair. His head nudged her palm when his lips closed around one nipple and he suckled it mercilessly.

"I missed you so . . ." he breathed, as he favored the other bud with the same treatment. Suddenly, his hands tightened on her hips and he hoisted her against the massive wall of his chest.

Rencia wiggled her feet out of the black leather-pumps, then curled her legs around Ivan's lean waist. She felt him walking and held on to his shoulders as her lips sought his in the darkness.

With an athlete's agility, Ivan held Rencia high above him and feasted on the soft flesh between and beneath her breasts. When he lifted her impossibly higher and kissed her navel, she squealed in delight. A second later, she felt the luxurious wine-colored down bed comforter beneath her back. Her eyes had adjusted to the darkness and she could see Ivan still standing as he disrobed.

The crisp, inviting covers were soon tangled around them as the friction of their bodies devoid of any clothing stimulated them beyond reason.

Ivan was like a man possessed, losing himself in the feel of Rencia's silken thighs and hair. His hands were everywhere, caressing and massaging her. When his fingers disappeared inside her panties, her need was evident.

Rencia turned her face into the pillow and chewed her

nail to avoid screaming at the scandalous pleasure over-
taking her. Ivan began a slow assault on her breasts once
more. His lips nibbled insistently as his fingers delved inside her body. Instinctively, Rencia's hips rose from the
bed only to be pressed back against the firm mattress. She
was immersed in a sea of emotion, feeling whatever resis-
tance she had ooze away. Just as the pleasure became
almost too much to bear, Ivan withdrew his fingers and replaced them with his stunning male length.

A low, tortured moan welled in Rencia's throat when
she felt him stretching the taut walls of her femininity.
Her hands weakened and rested on either side of her
head. Ivan laced his fingers between hers as his thrusts
slowed.

"Zhabi." She sighed, undulating her hips to match his
rhythm.

The sensual curve of his mouth twitched from satisfaction. "Hmm?" he replied, managing a chuckle when
she only moaned. Of course, he was just as far gone as
she. He ordered himself not to rush what was happening. This was a moment he intended to savor. He delved
into her body with deeper strokes that bathed his male-
ness in an increased wealth of moisture. He uttered a
ragged sound that was muffled in the crook of her neck
where he inhaled the fantastic scent of her perfume.

Rencia ached to touch him and strained against his
hands pressing hers into the covers. Still, the masterful
gesture only heightened her arousal. Ivan maintained
the unhurried lunges, loving the high-pitched cries she
uttered into the air. When she tried to nudge him into
increasing his speed, Ivan only pressed her thighs to the
bed and continued the leisurely assault.

Writhing like a lazy cat, Rencia took everything Ivan had
to give. When Ivan draped one of her legs across his shoul-

der and finally took her with quick, ravishing strokes, Rencia was so overwhelmed that it took only a few moments for a powerful orgasm to explode within her.

The lovers lay in a tangle of covers, arms, and legs. Ivan dozed off, cradling the woman he loved in his arms. Rencia relished the fact that the physical aspect of their relationship was the one area that needed no work. But if the closeness they enjoyed was meant to last, the troubled spots of their marriage would have to be addressed. She smiled as the strong steady beat of his heart thudded against her cheek. They would not lose each other again, she vowed.

When she awoke, it was morning and she found herself gazing into Ivan's dreamy dark eyes.

"Good afternoon," he greeted.

Rencia smiled and trailed her fingers down the side of his face. "Afternoon?"

"Mmm-hmm, it's after two P.M."

"What?" she cried, bolting upright in the bed. "How could you let me sleep so late?"

"I tried to wake you," he fibbed.

"Mmm-hmm," Rencia retorted, obviously unconvinced. "You know what everyone's gonna think," she groaned, flopping back down on the bed.

"Well, at least they'll be right," he teased, ducking when she hurled a pillow at him. "What?" he whispered, leaning close when he noticed the change in her expression.

Rencia managed a quick shake of her head. "Nothing," she lied.

"Baby, I'm sorry," Ivan apologized. "You just looked so peaceful and I figured you needed your sleep, so—"

"Oh, Zhabi, I don't mind. I feel great."

"Well then, what's wrong with you? Why did you look at me so strange a few seconds ago?"

Rencia's gaze softened. "A new year is coming and it hasn't been our best time and this has all been so wonderful," she said, her voice holding just a trace of regret.

Ivan noticed. He left the bed and walked over to the large easy chair and took a seat. Placing his elbow on the arm of the chair, he propped his chin in his hand and watched her.

"What?" Rencia asked after a moment, questioning the unnerving dark stare.

"Everything."

Rencia sighed and leaned back against the headboard. "What are we gonna do about it?"

"Talk?"

"We tried that. Many, many times."

"Talk to each other, not at each other, Larry. Talk about it all from the beginning, from where things really started to go wrong."

Rencia focused on the black carpet. "All I wanted to do was work, Zhabi," she said in a blunt tone.

Ivan closed his eyes. "I know."

"Then why'd it all have to be so hard back then?" she asked, still watching the carpet.

"'Cause I was cruel and selfish and a caveman," he said, bringing a smile to Rencia's face. "But there were a couple of other reasons too."

Rencia remained silent and waited for him to continue.

Ivan closed his eyes. He knew he could do this. For so long he'd been afraid to appear weak or fearful before her. Now he knew that she was the only one he wanted to share his fears with. "Up until I was six," he began, "my pop was working in Atlanta in a steel plant. He and my Ma and me lived in a shack. That's making it sound good."

"You still remember it?"

"I could never forget it. Anyway, um . . ." Ivan paused for a second to clear his throat. "Ma worked to help keep food on the table."

Rencia smiled. "Zhabi, I know all this."

"Yeah, but you don't know that Ma was pregnant with another child after me. She lost it."

Rencia let out a shaky breath. "Oh God, Zhabi—"

He raised one hand. "When that happened, Pop forbade her to ever work again. She didn't take it too well, and to make things worse, my father blamed her for the loss. I had never been so scared in my life. I just knew they were gonna split up. It took a long time for them to get back what they had. But I think the only reason they lasted was that she did things his way. No arguments."

Rencia left the bed and knelt before him. "Sweetie, I'm so sorry. No wonder you were so . . . Baby, we're not your folks. We never will be."

"We still lost our baby," he reminded her softly.

"I know," she whispered, a lone tear escaping her eyes to trickle down her cheek. "I was so busy. I didn't take my fatigue and edginess as signs that I should see my doctor. Nothing's ever hurt me as much as losing our baby, Zhabi. You have to know that."

"I do," he assured her, tugging on a curl of her hair. "I think all I could see was the way Pop looked whenever he talked about Mama and the baby they lost. I didn't even realize how much of what happened during that time of my life still affected me. When I was in the same position and could feel the pain firsthand, it almost killed me. Men feel that stuff too, Larry."

Rencia nodded, smoothing her hand over Ivan's hair. "I know, but, honey, this tore us apart."

Ivan nodded as well. "For a very long time."

"And counting."

"Now we've got different lives, different interests," he interjected smoothly.

Rencia knew where he was coming from. "That may be true, but one thing hasn't changed. I'm still in love with my husband," she vowed.

"Your husband is still in love with you," he replied, smiling at her. Then his expression became serious. "Larry, I need to hear you say you believe that I didn't have sex with Hester."

Rencia chuckled then and shook her head. "I know that, Zhabi. I think I realized that as soon as I had a chance to step back and look at the situation. I know you wouldn't do that to me . . . to us. Hester was a scheming slut and she doesn't matter."

Ivan's dark brows drew closed as he smiled. "An enemy, Larry? I'm impressed."

"Don't be," Rencia advised with a wave of her hand. "Hester's not worth the effort it would take to hate her. I'll take care of her."

"How?"

"Don't worry about it."

Ivan watched her for a long while before he shrugged. "You think we can get back some semblance of what we had before all this mess happened?"

Rencia slid her arms around his neck. "It's a lot of mess to work through," she warned him. "Our hurt feelings aren't gonna just vanish after all this time, but I want what we had too."

"It'll be tough living in New York and New Jersey," he pointed out.

Rencia shrugged one shoulder. "Well, I'm getting tired of livin' alone and—"

"You'll come back home with me?" Ivan finished for her, his eyes widening slightly.

"Do you want me to?"

"Don't ask stupid questions," he said, lowering his mouth to hers. In one effortless motion, he scooped her onto his lap.

Her hands smoothed across his wide, sleek chest as they kissed deeply. The sheet slipped past Rencia's chest, and Ivan's long lashes closed briefly over his eyes when he glimpsed the full, luscious globes. When he bowed his head and filled his mouth with her, she threw her head back and gasped.

Suddenly, he stopped and raised his head to fix her with an intense look.

"What is it?"

"I love you. With everything in me, I love you," Ivan whispered fiercely.

Rencia kissed his neck and smiled, feeling more content that ever. "I love you too, Zhabi."

They were silent for a long while, simply enjoying being in each other's arms.

Chapter Twenty-two

One week after Christmas, Rencia arrived at GeFran Cosmetics feeling refreshed and optimistic. Dropping her gray leather briefcase to her desk, she decided to pay Geneva a visit while everything was still relatively calm. Geneva wasn't in her office, but Hester was there speaking to Lola Sheridan.

"Girl, you are so lucky to have Rencia in your corner," Lola was saying.

"Hmph," Hester replied, rolling her eyes.

Lola frowned. "What? She *did* get you a nude spread in *GC*, didn't she? They've never given a black model a ten-page layout."

"Forget that green-eyed bitch. I would've gotten that job myself sooner or later."

"Hester—"

"Uh-uh, Lola. I'm sick of it always bein' about Rencia. Rencia this and Rencia that. Rencia's so wonderful and sweet and beautiful," she mocked. "Oooh! I want to vomit every time I see her."

Lola shook her head. "Damn, I can't believe you work so well with her," she marveled, only now realizing her friend's extreme dislike for the woman.

A devious smirk crossed Hester's mouth. "Well, I fixed her ass good when we were all in Atlantic City." She told

Lola about her scheme that resulted with her and Ivan in bed together.

Lola rolled her eyes when she'd finished. "Lord, Hester, that was so stupid. Don't you know they're tryin' to get back together?"

Hester waved her hand. "Forget 'em," she stated simply.

Rencia shook her head and leaned against the wall. Hearing Hester admit what she'd done filled her with an indescribable rage . . . and even more desire to go through with her plans.

"Good morning," Rencia called to Hester and Lola when she finally stepped into the office. Lola greeted her nervously while Hester remained silent.

Rencia circled Geneva's desk, trailing the tip of one nail along the oak top. "Lola, I've been trying to get in touch with you all morning."

Lola sent Hester a nervous glance before looking back at Rencia. "Why?"

"What are you doing for lunch?"

Lola shook her head. "Nothing." Her dark face beamed with expectancy.

Rencia picked up the phone and dialed.

"David Milner's office," a friendly voice answered.

"Hi, Michelle, what's up?" Rencia spoke lightly to David's secretary, Michelle Laurels.

"Oh, hey, Rencia. Girl, I'm just waiting for five o'clock," she teased.

Rencia chuckled. "I hear ya. Listen, tell David that Lola Sheridan is free for lunch."

"Will do," Michelle promised.

"Thanks, 'Schelle," Rencia replied, before replacing the receiver.

Lola's pretty brown eyes were wide as she took a step closer to the desk. "Rencia, what's going on?"

"David Milner and I have decided to use you for the first *GC* spread."

"What?" Hester cried.

Rencia continued, "He and his associates weren't altogether happy with their previous choice. Soon as I showed 'em your portfolio, they were hooked, Lola."

"Oh my Lord, I can't believe this," Lola whispered, placing her hand across her chest.

Rencia shrugged. "Well, they love your look and they're willing to offer you the shoot if you still think you can handle a nude layout."

"Yes, I can handle it!" Lola exclaimed. Rushing around the desk, she hugged Rencia and kissed her cheek. "Thanks, Rencia, thank you so much!"

"Think of it as a belated Christmas gift."

"Oh, I gotta go! I have so much to do," she called, tearing out of the office.

"We're meeting at the Seasons. One o'clock sharp!"

Hester stood across the room stone-faced and livid. "Letting your personal feelings interfere with your work? . . . Not very professional."

A hateful smirk tugged at Rencia's mouth. "Well, now you know how it feels."

Hester walked closer to the desk. "I knew you weren't as syrupy sweet as you had everybody thinking."

"And I should've known you're nothing more than a scheming whore."

Hester winced. "Bitch," she spat.

"And don't you ever forget it," Rencia cooly advised, stepping from behind the desk to stroll toward the office door.

Hester hurried after her. "You can't do this! That spread was mine!"

Rencia shrugged and turned around to face her. "Well, like you just told Lola, you could've gotten it yourself sooner or later."

"You can't do this," Hester groaned.

"It's done," Rencia assured her, her perfect brows rising sharply.

Hester clenched her fists, pressing her lips together as she tried to hide her tears. Failing miserably, she ran from the office.

Only a few days remained until the arrival of the new year. Shortly after returning from London, Ivan and Rencia settled back into married life. When she wasn't working, Rencia spent her time interviewing candidates to assume the lease on her condo. She hadn't realized how much she'd missed their Brooklyn brownstone until she moved back in. Their professional careers charged along full steam, but now they supported each other 100 percent. Things were returning to normal. For the most part.

Rencia eased the pink-flowered cardboard box back into her closet and replaced the five shoe boxes on top of it before pushing the door shut. She had purchased the innocent-looking box for one purpose: to store a pharmacist's supply of home pregnancy tests.

It was a habit she'd taken to since she and Ivan had resumed their sexual relationship full-time. Though she was taking birth-control pills, she knew there was still the possibility of pregnancy and faithfully tested herself when her period was even a day late.

As strongly Rencia tried to stifle them, the old fears always resurfaced. *What if I am? Will I lose this one too? What will Zhabi think?*

Raking all ten fingers through her disheveled curls, she checked the wall clock. Then, tentatively, she stepped closer to the slender instrument lying atop a paper towel on the counter. She'd prepared herself over a dozen times, it seemed. None of that was relevant, however, when she saw the double blue stripe indicating a positive response.

A heavy tuft of air felt lodged in her throat, before it was expelled by some unseen force. Her eyes grew wide as she gave the plastic stick a reflexive shake as though the action would somehow change the results. She was able to move only as far as the toilet, where she sat on the closed cover and stared off into space.

"Larry?"

Ivan's voice was amplified when he repeated his call while walking into the bedroom. Her heart racing at a more frantic pace, Rencia grabbed the paper towel and wrapped it around the plastic tube before tossing everything into the wastebasket.

"In here, Zhabi!" she called, standing before the mirrored wall and pretending to fuss with her hair.

Ivan pulled her back against his chest, burying his gorgeous face into the crook of her neck. "Mmm," he growled, his hands moving to untie her robe's belt and disappearing beneath the white linen to cup her breasts.

Rencia's head settled back against his shoulder. She felt faint, trapped amidst triple emotions of happiness, unease, and arousal.

For Ivan, her response increased his own arousal. The feel of her body beneath his hands was indescribable. At last, he made her face him, his mouth gliding along the flawless line of her neck.

"God, I'm so glad you're home," he breathed, inhaling her scent. His arms tightened like steel bands around her waist.

Rencia responded with a breathless giggle. "Well, I've been back for a while, you know?"

"And I'm still glad," he declared, his kisses gaining pressure.

Rencia dismissed the feelings of unease and savored the feel of her husband's touch. In seconds, the robe was on the floor and she was in his arms as they headed out of the bathroom. Ivan lost what little restraint he had and quickly released himself from the confines of his belt and sagging jeans.

Rencia gasped his name when he held her against the doorjamb and took her with lengthy, heated thrusts. Her long legs locked around his back and she begged him to never stop.

Later that afternoon, Rencia was roused from a light slumber by the feel of soft kisses bathing her shoulder blades.

"Hungry?" Ivan asked, when she turned over to face him.

Her eyes closed lazily. "I could eat a little something," she admitted with a smile.

Ivan kissed the tip of her nose. "I'll be back," he said, leaving the bed to stroll naked from the room.

The lazy, contented look vanished from Rencia's face. She waited for the sound of his footsteps to soften on the stairway, then reached for the phone on the nightstand.

"Dr. Kenneth Lentz's office. This is Samantha."

"Hi, Samantha, this is Lawrencia DeZhabi."

"Hey, Rencia!" Samantha Cates greeted, pleased to be

speaking with the doctor's most famous patient. "What can we do for you today?"

Rencia cleared her throat and glanced toward the bedroom door. "I, um, I need to make an appointment."

"Okay," Samantha drawled in a southern accent, as she pulled up the patient file on her computer. "Is everything all right?"

"Oh, fine, fine. I, um, I just need to confirm the results of a home pregnancy test."

"I see," Samantha said, the look on her round face harboring disappointment as her blue eyes scanned the screen. "Well, sweetie, I hate to tell you this, but with the holidays and all—"

"I know," Rencia whispered, glancing toward the bedroom door again, "I just really want to confirm these results ASAP."

Samantha smiled to herself. "I understand, hon. I could suggest a referral. Someone discreet in light of who you are."

"I appreciate that, Samantha, but—"

"I understand," Samantha noted with a quick nod. "Forget I mentioned it. Let's go on and get you an appointment set up, and should the doctor have a cancelation you'll be the first person I call."

"Thanks, Samantha." Rencia sighed, her edginess somewhat abated.

Ivan strolled back into the bedroom, finding Rencia sitting up with the covers tucked around her. He carried a tray laden with two bowls of grapes, sliced bananas, apples, two huge blueberry muffins, and two large glasses of orange juice.

"Good work." Rencia applauded and reached over for a muffin.

During the course of their afternoon munching, Ivan

glimpsed his wife's face and took note of her faraway expression.

"What's up?" he inquired, popping a grape into his mouth.

Rencia adopted a dreamy look then. "Sometimes it just seems so unreal to be back together now after being apart for so long. So much has happened between us, you know? she said, reaching out to caress the strong curve of his jaw. "It's just like a dream being here."

Ivan set his juice aside and reached out to cup her face. "It's no dream," he assured her, his thumbs brushing the corner of her mouth before he pulled her in for a brief kiss.

"Zhabi, I—"

"What?" he murmured, when she cut herself off.

"I pray we hold on to each other this time," she said, deciding against telling him about the test.

"We will," he promised softly, nuzzling his face against her temple.

Rencia locked her arms about his neck and held him tight. Her eyes glistened with tears as she stared up at the ceiling.

The new Breeze campaign had gotten off to a roaring start in the new year.

Ivan and Rencia's magazine layouts were a definite rage and the possibility of television spots had even been discussed. Ivan found it hard to believe they had caused such a stir. Rencia found much amusement in observing her husband's reaction to his new found celebrity status.

"I'm flattered and you people know that, since it's all I've been saying since this whole thing started."

The GeFran executives chuckled, appreciating Ivan's

modesty. The group met not only to celebrate another milestone in the Breeze line, but also to hail the arrival of a new year.

"Still," Ivan added, tapping his fingers against the tablecloth, "I think I'll be leaving this side of the business to my wife. I don't think I want to stomach the craziness TV exposure would bring."

"Well, I guess that seals it," Silas Timmons said. "Rencia's already dedicated herself to fulfilling her role as Destiny/GeFran's scheduling director. We were hoping you could change her mind, Ivan," he added, watching the man give a decisive wave of his hand.

"So this is definitely the end of the Breeze couple?" Frank Arnold asked.

Rencia blinked and focused on his handsome face. Her eyes began to sting with the sudden pressure of tears.

"Oooh." Geneva gestured with a quick knock against the dining table. "My emotions are about to get the better of me. Care to dance, Mr. Arnold?" she asked, standing when Frank extended his hand.

The other guests at the table followed suit. Soon, the DeZhabis were left alone.

"Are you two ready to place your orders or would you prefer to wait for the others?"

Ivan smiled up at the waitress before sending Rencia a quick wink. "How 'bout it?" he asked. "Babe?" he called again when she didn't respond. He finally leaned in to whisper, "Larry?" before snapping his fingers before her face. It took several seconds before she blinked and watched him curiously.

Slowly, Ivan looked back up at the server. "I think we'll wait," he decided, watching the smiling brunette walk away before he turned back to Rencia. "Tell me what's wrong."

"I'm sorry, Zhabi. I just drifted off there for a minute."

"You been doin' a lot of that over the last few days."

"Yeah." She sighed, taking a long swallow of water to soothe her dry throat, "A lot's been goin' on and I've been so out of it."

"And that's it?" Ivan persisted, still not completely convinced.

Rencia fidgeted with the tassels on her empire-waisted top. "What Frank said got to me, I guess. About this being the end of the Breeze couple," she clarified, watching him nod. "I guess I took it a bit too literally."

"Larry," he groaned, covering her hand with his.

"Zhabi, do you think we'll make it this time?"

Ivan was stunned by the question. "Hey," he whispered, taking her hands and making her face him. "What is this? You having doubts about us?"

"No, I'm very happy and very excited about us." She smoothed her hand across the worsted fabric of his cream suit coat.

Ivan caught her hand. "Then why do I feel like there's more going on here? I've seen you drifting off and looking so sad, so many times over the past few days, and I wonder if it really has anything to do with—"

Rencia looked out over the enchanting décor of the restaurant, which was complete with a stunning view of Manhattan from its top-floor location. "It's the beginning of another year, Zhabi. I'm just sort of uptight about it, I guess."

"Hey, listen to me," Ivan soothed, leaned forward to press his forehead against hers. "Yes, it is a new year and we're new. New and determined not to lose what we have. Not to take it for granted. You believe that, don't you?"

Rencia had scooted close and interrupted his words with a kiss that silenced all his questions. They were caught up in the midst of it when their dinner companions returned to the table.

"All right, break it up!" Geneva ordered.

Laughter followed and the evening continued wonderfully.

"I really appreciate this, Samantha."

Samantha Cates smiled at the deep remorse filling Lawrencia's voice. "For the fifth time, it's no problem. You have every right to be eager to get this done."

Rencia massaged her forehead. "Thanks for understanding."

"Anytime. Now, we'll see you tomorrow, okay?"

"All right," Rencia promised, her voice still shaking terribly. She squeezed her hands to stop their trembling once she'd replaced the receiver. She was chanting the words "calm down" when Ivan walked into the kitchen.

"Hey, Larry," he greeted sweetly. His soft deep voice held the slightest trace of unease as though he were uncertain how she would respond to him.

"Hey," Rencia called in the detached manner she'd adopted during the past week.

Ivan pulled open the refrigerator door, but stared unseeingly at the array of food. His wife's absent, pre-occupied behavior toward him had forced him to accept what he feared most. In spite of what she'd said, the time apart had caused irreparable damage, and her feelings toward their having a real marriage had changed.

Rencia cleared her throat and shuffled over to the mahogany cabinets. "What do you have the taste for tonight?" she asked, shoving her hands into the back pocket of her jeans.

"Leave dinner to me," he said, pushing the refrigerator door closed. "Come on." He took her hand to lead her out into the living room.

"Zhabi, you don't have to do this."

Ivan pressed a kiss to the back of her hand. "I want to," he said, turning to face her. "Listen, I want you to get some rest or take a bath while I cook."

Standing on the tips of her sandals, Rencia kissed his cheek. "I appreciate being pampered, but I don't need it."

"I think we both know that you do," he whispered, knowing she couldn't deny it. "Go relax, I'll come get you when I'm done," he promised, pressing a kiss to her forehead. His soft expression turned weary and uncertain as he watched her ascend the stairs.

Ivan was securing his twisted locks into a ponytail when he heard the front door slam.

"Larry?" he called, but there was no response.

After a brief hesitation, he grabbed his keys and sprinted downstairs. He opened the door in time to see Rencia pulling her car out of her parking space in front of their brownstone.

Ivan kept a close yet discreet tail on his wife through the heavy flow of downtown traffic. He watched her park inside one of the garages, then followed her to a brick office building across the street. Once inside the crowded high-rise, he lost her.

"Damn," he muttered. *Where could she be going?* he pondered, then decided to check the building directory.

Only one name stood out among the list of white block-lettered entries: Dr. Kenneth Lentz.

"Larry," he whispered, his confusion turning to concern.

Ivan located the doctor's office in record time. He walked into the bright, lavender-painted room and waited in line behind two pregnant ladies. His wife at the forefront of his thoughts, he was oblivious to all the interested stares he received from the women waiting to be examined.

"Mr. DeZhabi," Samantha greeted, recognizing him immediately from the ads with his wife. "Mrs. DeZhabi just went in."

Ivan feigned a look of relief. "I thought I'd missed her," he said, hiding the fact that he had no idea why Rencia was there.

"Well, I know you're both quite excited," Samantha said as she stood behind the white counter. "Confirming these results shouldn't take long at all. Let me take you back," she offered, already stepping out into the waiting area.

"You know," Ivan called, barely able to hear his own voice above his heart pounding in his ears, "I'll just let her see the doctor alone. If you could just tell her I was here and that I'll see her back home."

"If you prefer." Samantha obliged, though a curious light shone in her brown eyes.

"Thanks," Ivan told her, forcing a smile when Samantha escorted him to the doctor's private exit.

As he headed back home, Ivan's mind raced with questions and uncertainties. Was she pregnant? Was that the explanation for her distant mood? Why didn't she tell him? Would this pregnancy turn out like the last?

Hell, fool, you have to know why she'd keep this a secret! Ivan berated himself, pounding a fist against his palm. He couldn't help but remember how coldly he'd reacted after the miscarriage. *But does she think I'd still react that way?* he asked himself. *Surely she knows I'm past those feelings, or does she?*

Rencia took her time returning home when Samantha had given her Ivan's message. How did he find her there? she wondered.

"Oh well." She sighed, smoothing both hands across the front of her stylish denim dress. "May as well go in and ask the source."

Nothing prepared her for the sight that met her eyes when she walked through the front door of their home. It was a frosty January evening and in the center of their spacious living room was a glittering ball that cast a shimmering sparkle of lights to every corner. The floor was littered with balloons. Soft jazzy tunes drifted from the state-of-the-art CD changer in the corner of the room.

"Zhabi? . . ."

Suddenly, two arms encircled her waist and she was drawn against the warm, solid wall of Ivan's chest.

"Happy New Year's," he murmured against her neck.

"You're a bit late. Why did you do this? *When* did you find time to do this?"

"I remembered something you said about our past New Year's being so awful."

Rencia bowed her head to hide her disappointment. "I'm afraid this one won't be much better. Obviously you did this because of my appointment."

"Larry—"

"I'm not pregnant."

Ivan focused on his white Nikes visible beneath his khaki trousers. "Why'd you make an appointment?"

"I took a test at home first," she said, as she strolled farther into the room. "I guess that's why those things aren't one hundred percent accurate." Nervous laughter colored her words.

Ivan wasn't amused.

"Anyway," she continued, wanting him to know everything, "I've been testing myself almost every month for a while now."

"Why'd you keep it from me?" Ivan questioned, seeming stunned by her confession.

She couldn't look at him. "I don't know."

"I think you do," he softly accused, watching her lean against the arm of the sofa and groan into her hands. "I thought everything had been hashed out and resolved before we left London. But that's not true, is it?"

Rencia shook her head and looked down, curls curtaining her face as she did so. "There was . . . something. Something I didn't want to get into."

Ivan sat up in his chair and folded his arms across the front of his black Karl Kani T-shirt. "Can you get into it now?"

Rencia massaged her neck. "I suppose I've waited too long already."

"I'm listening."

"I actually didn't talk about this in London, because I—I didn't realize it was even still an issue until that test came out positive."

"What happened then?"

Rencia looked at him then. "Zhabi, I couldn't help but think about a miscarriage and what would happen if I lost the baby—another baby." A sob built in her throat. "But this time, this time it wouldn't be because I worked too hard or because I didn't notice the signs. It would happen simply because it wasn't meant for us to have a child. Ever."

"And you couldn't say that to me?" Ivan whispered, disbelief coming to his face. "Do you know what was goin' through my mind, Larry? I thought you were having regrets about us being back together."

"Never. No, Zhabi, never that," Rencia swore, placing both hands against her chest. "But all I could think about was what happened before and the way—"

Ivan pressed her lips together. "The way I acted?"

"The way things just got out of control."

Ivan suddenly closed the distance between them. Bounding toward the table, he clasped her hands between his and pulled her before him.

"Don't you know that you're enough for me?" he whispered, giving her hands a tiny shake. "You've always been enough," he stressed, his voice becoming hoarse with emotion. "Even before everything that happened . . . having a child together would've been another fantastic thing to happen for us, but I never should've let you think it was something I had to have or couldn't live without, I admit it. I want kids, very much. But without you . . ." He stepped closer, pressing his forehead against hers. "Baby, I love you and what I want most is for you to believe we are meant to last and that I want you—I want us. Just the way we are."

Tears filled Rencia's eyes, bluring her vision before they spilled down her flawless cheeks. Her nails traced Ivan's mouth as though she were hoping to capture the beautiful words he had just spoken.

"Is this all, Larry?" he whispered, when her eyes met his. "Are you . . . holding anything back? *Anything* else you need to say to me?"

Rencia blinked, forcing the remaining tears from her eyes. "I don't think so," she told him, stroking the strong cords in his neck. "I believe everything you said, Zhabi, but even that won't quell the fears sure to rise when another test comes out positive."

Nodding, Ivan brushed his thumbs along the slope of her nose. "I understand that, but promise you'll talk to me whenever you're afraid. Come to me anytime, Larry. Don't shut me out. It scares me and I can't handle it."

"I promise," she vowed, smiling as she searched his dark eyes with her light ones. She loved him even more for being so forthright with his feelings.

"And promise me somethin' else?"

"Anything."

"I want to be there every time you take one of these tests."

"Okay."

Ivan kissed her long and deep then. It was more than just a physical reward, it was a seal to consummate the words and promises they had spoken. When he pulled away, his smile was naughty and playful.

"So." He sighed, his thumbs caressing her cheeks as he pressed his forehead against hers, "in order for me to be there for the test, you're gonna need a reason to take one, right?"

Recognizing the mischief in his deep-set stare, Rencia giggled. "I guess," she said, laughing.

Ivan drew her even closer to him. "Then let me give you one." He growled into her neck, his hands closing over her hips as he drew her down to the furry hunter-green carpet before the fireplace.

Rencia's soft laughter mingled with the sounds of the exquisite melodies filling the atmosphere. For the first time in so long she was filled with a complete sense of hope and happiness, due in no small part to the solidity of her marriage. Still, it was the promise of a new year that elated her. At last she could look forward to a future brimming with all the things she had prayed for: passion, support, and love—the most important elements of marriage and the things she planned to share with her husband forever.

Dear Readers,

I've treasured your support and encouraging words following my debut novels. Thank you so much for choosing to spend your time and money on my work. Knowing that so many of you have enjoyed these books and possess such passionate views on the characters and storylines has made my introduction to the writing world more exciting than I ever dreamed it would be. *Finding Love Again* presents married couple Ivan and Lawrencia DeZhabi. I pray you all found them to be a passionate couple—not only in the physical sense, but also in the way they related to one another as they faced such tremendous obstacles.

As always, I look forward to your comments as they enable me to cultivate my craft. E-mail me: altonya@writeme.com.

Peace and Blessings,
AlTonya R. Washington

ABOUT THE AUTHOR

AlTonya Washington is the author of *Remember Love* and *Guarded Love*. Both novels were released in 2003. She's a fan of both the contemporary and the historical romance genres. A South Carolina native, she currently resides there, where she works as a library reference associate.